"I am not trying to pick a fight, I'm—"

"No?" Simon's voice was sneering as he interrupted her. "You're certainly giving a good imitation, then."

"As I was saying," Cassie went on through gritted teeth, "I'm merely trying to find out if there is any possibility whatsoever of us having even a semblance of a social life. Do I accept this party invitation or not?"

Simon sighed. "I've already told you, love, I just can't leave at the moment. This project is my baby, Cassie, and I have to be on hand to see it through. Look, why don't you come up this weekend, and I'll meet you in Glasgow and we'll—"

"No, I won't," Cassie shot back angrily. "If it's too much effort for you to try to get home, then why the hell should I bother?" And she slammed down the phone.

SALLY
WENTWORTH

semi-detached marriage

Harlequin Books

TORONTO • NEW YORK • LOS ANGELES • LONDON
AMSTERDAM • PARIS • SYDNEY • HAMBURG
STOCKHOLM • ATHENS • TOKYO • MILAN

Harlequin Presents first edition October 1982
ISBN 0-373-10542-8

Original hardcover edition published in 1982
by Mills & Boon Limited

CHAPTER ONE

THERE was a queue at the check-out at the supermarket, and Cassandra Ventris tapped her foot impatiently as she waited her turn. *Come on*, get a move on, can't you? But the woman at the head of the line was fussily packing her groceries neatly into her shopping bags as if she had all the time in the world, whereas Cassie had to get home and cook the main course for tonight's dinner party as well as do the table and get herself ready before seven-thirty. She glanced again at her watch; it was almost six now. If that darned woman at the front didn't get a move on she'd still be arranging the table when the guests arrived. She'd meant to do it this morning, of course, but there hadn't been time. No matter how organised she was, there still never seemed to be time. At last the woman was paying and moving away, and Cassie gave a sigh of relief as the other two people in front of her got quickly through and she was able to empty her own wire basket and hastily pack the things in a couple of plastic bags.

Outside the supermarket the February winds made her shiver and she pulled her coat close around her, feeling the cold even more after the warmth of the shop. Luckily she only had to walk a few hundred yards to the flat and she hurried along, a tall, slim figure in her belted black coat and high-heeled boots, the winds teasing out tendrils of chestnut hair from the neat, upswept style she'd worn to work.

The flat was on the second floor of a largish block in

St John's Wood. From the outside the building didn't look very attractive, but the flats were large and airy, there was ample parking and a small square of grass and trees outside, and, most important of all, it was conveniently situated on the outskirts of central London within walking distance of an Underground station.

Cassie didn't bother with the lift but hurried up the two flights of stairs, trying to carry the shopping and fumble for the bunch of keys in her bag at the same time. She found them, but had to put down the shopping bags outside the door while she picked out the right one. There were letters on the mat behind the door, but beyond stooping to pick them up and put them on the hall table she ignored them; they would have to wait.

'Simon?' She called her husband's name in the faint hope that he might have got home early, but the flat was silent, there was no answering call. She hurried to the kitchen, dropping her coat on a chair on the way, and hurriedly began to prepare the main course, rolling out a piece of ready-made pastry in which to wrap the fillet of beef, putting it in the oven and getting the vegetables ready to put on later. The first course and the dessert were to be cold, and she'd cheated and bought them already made the day before. It wasn't that she couldn't cook; she'd learnt the basics at school and had taken an evening class course on continental cookery when she and Simon had got engaged, but there just wasn't the time to mess about with long complicated recipes. And besides, the practical side of her rebelled at spending hours preparing a dish that would be eaten in about twenty minutes with nothing left to show for it but a pile of washing up that would take another hour to clear. Or at least it would have done if she hadn't insisted that they lash out on a dishwasher soon after they'd moved in.

With the meat cooking, Cassie was able to give her attention to the rest of·the flat. At least it was clean and tidy, she could be sure that Mrs Payne, their cleaning woman, had seen to that. Although she had rather eccentric ideas about punctuality and was not above helping herself to a drop of gin to keep out the cold or the heat, depending on the season, she was an energetic worker and was indispensable in the smooth running of their lives. Not that Cassie ever saw her very much, because she had always left for work before Mrs Payne arrived and didn't get home until after she'd gone. She was just an invisible good fairy who came twice a week and left notes in prominent places if she needed anything—an arrangement that worked very well so long as the gin didn't run out.

The flat was carpeted throughout in deep-pile creamy white and had very modern furniture. The walls, too, were painted white, but one whole wall in the living room was given over to bookshelves and racks of records, and there were several pictures on the walls and lots of brightly coloured and oddly-shaped cushions on the long, low settee. There was also a big red leather chesterfield which Cassie didn't particularly like but which Simon had insisted on bringing with him from his parents' home. It was quite old and rather scratched, and there were scuff marks on one arm because Simon always put his feet up on it while he was watching television. There were two bedrooms with a bathroom in between, a kitchen and hall, as well as the big living room which had the dining table at the far end set into a bay formed by the windows overlooking the square of garden. In summer it was pleasant to look out at the trees and you could almost imagine you were out in the country if it wasn't for the hum of the traffic, but now Cassie pulled the heavy velvet curtains shut and turned on all the lights while she put the mats and cutlery on the glass-topped table.

While she worked she played back the cassette on the answer-phone, listening to the messages. There was one from a local firm with an estimate for new fitted wardrobes in the main bedroom, and another in her mother's terse voice issuing an invitation-cum-command to visit them on her father's birthday. Cassie smiled when she heard it; her mother hated speaking to the answer-phone machine and it had taken ages before she'd been persuaded not to ring off and keep trying until she found them at home. But then she'd realised how useful it could be when she wanted Cassie to do something she might not want to without being able to argue back, and had consented to use the device. A third call was from her dentist confirming the time of an appointment, and then Simon's familiar voice, crisp and authoritative, even though hurried: 'I'm sorry, darling, but something's cropped up and I may be later getting home than I'd hoped. Should be able to make it, though, if all goes well; I'll phone you if I can't, of course. Don't forget to put the wine to chill, if I'm not there on time. 'Bye, darling. See you.'

Cassie's brows drew into a frown of annoyance. Not again! Lately it seemed as though every time they made arrangements to entertain or to go out Simon was kept late at the office. Still, as he'd pointed out, she'd known when she married him that his job as troubleshooter for a large industrial concern would be very demanding, keeping him late to try and solve problems over the phone or, if there was an emergency, sending him almost anywhere in the world at a moment's notice. And just now his company was having some trouble with a new oil terminal they were building in Scotland, and Simon had his hands full trying to deal with it.

The clock in the hall struck the hour and Cassie hurriedly checked on the roast before going into the bathroom for a quick shower, turning the radio on so that she could listen to the music on Radio Two. She dressed and made up again quickly, brushing her long chestnut hair and arranging it with deft, practised hands by parting it in the middle and taking a lock back from either side and fastening it at the back, like a girl in a Pre-Raphaelite painting. A long-sleeved crushed velvet dress in deep red and soft, delicate make-up that emphasised her eyes increased the illusion, but Cassie only wasted a second on a critical look at herself in the mirror before hurrying back to the kitchen to put an apron over her dress while she did the vegetables and put the wine to cool.

As she did so she heard Simon's key in the lock and he called out to her as he hurried through to the bedroom. Cassie glanced at the clock on the cooker—seven-twenty-five. With any luck the guests would be a few minutes late and she would have enough time to arrange the flowers she'd bought on the way home. She had just finished and placed the centrepiece on the table when the bell rang. Taking off the apron, she threw it into the kitchen, took a last glance at herself in the mirror in the hall as she smoothed her dress, then opened the door with a serene, welcoming smile, as if she had had all the time in the world.

The first couple to arrive were Sue and Christopher Martin, as Cassie had guessed they would be. They hadn't been to the flat before as Sue had only begun to

work at Marriott & Brown's, the big London department store where Cassie was a fashion buyer, a few
months ago, although their friendship had developed
straight away. Also the couple were younger and were
newly married, so weren't sure enough of themselves
to arrive more than a few minutes late.

Cassie took their coats and led them into the sitting-
room, accepting the pot plant they'd brought for her
and their compliments on the room with genuine
pleasure. She had met Christopher Martin only once
before, at the store's annual Christmas party, and he
seemed nice enough, quite good-looking and about her
own age of twenty-four.

'What would you like to drink?'

'Have you got gin and tonic?'

'Yes, of course. How about you, Christopher?'

'Oh, make it Chris, please. Christopher always
sounds like something from a child's nursery song: you
know, "Christopher Robin went down with Alice" or
something. Hardly my scene at all. I can't think why
my mother chose the name. I always wanted to change
it, but everyone insists on making me stick to it.'

He said it rather brashly and Cassie wondered
whether he did it to draw attention to himself or just
to make himself appear older. 'Chris, then. What
would you like?'

'Vodka, please.'

'Anything with it?'

'No, just as it comes.'

Cassie moved to the drinks tray to pour it and handed
it to Chris just as Simon came into the room, and
immediately Christopher Martin seemed very young
and gauche, an overgrown schoolboy by comparison.

Simon crossed to her side and slipped an arm round

her waist as he bent to kiss her, his eyes smiling down
at her. 'Hi there.'

'Hi.'

He had changed into a dark blue velvet jacket that
sat well on his broad shoulders and there was a match-
ing bow tie at the neck of his crisp white shirt. He
looked casual and yet elegant, and no one would have
guessed that he had arrived home to shower and change
only a quarter of an hour ago. Neither of the Martins
had met him before, because he had been away at the
time of the Christmas party, and it gave Cassie a smug
little glow of satisfaction as she saw Sue's eyes widen
as she took in his tall, athletic figure and the dark,
saturnine handsomeness of his features. They had been
married for three years and dating for almost a year
before that, but Cassie still got that thrill of pleasure
when she saw another woman's eyes light with envy or
admiration on seeing him. She introduced him and
went to get him a whisky and soda while he sat down in an
armchair and talked to the Martins.

Cassie handed him his drink and perched on the arm
of his chair. He leant back, his long legs stuck out in
front of him and crossed at the ankles, completely at
ease. Cassie put a hand on his shoulder and he auto-
matically lifted his free hand to cover hers, playing
absently with her fingers while he drew Chris Martin
out to talk about his job. But even here the authority
in his manner came through; Chris recognised it at
once and spoke to him in a deferring tone, even
though Simon was only about eight years older.

'And you?' Chris was asking him. 'What do you
do?'

'Oh, I'm a general dogsbody for the Mullaine
Group. I have to try and sort out the problems with

their various subsidiary companies,' Simon answered lightly.

'Mullaine's—I've heard of them. They've got interests all over the world, haven't they?'

'Yes,' Simon admitted, 'I get around quite a bit.'

The bell rang, interrupting the conversation, and they both got up to welcome their last guests, Julia and John Russell, who were old friends, having been neighbours of Cassie's parents before her marriage. They were more Simon's age and John was almost as successful in his own line of business as Simon was. He had started his own textile manufacturing company soon after leaving university and, after some initial setbacks, had built it up into a thriving business that specialised in unusual fabrics for the up-market dress manufacturers. So, in a roundabout way, he and Cassie were both in the rag trade and often helped one another if they had the opportunity, John by letting Cassie know if he'd supplied material for garments he thought she might be interested in and Cassie by recommending John to the manufacturers she bought from, an arrangement that had often been advantageous to both of them.

They sat down to dinner quite shortly afterwards, and Cassie was pleased to see that her guests seemed to get on well, John teasing Sue a little so that she laughed and flushed and Julia being gracious to Chris when she wasn't passing on the latest bits of scandal to Cassie. Simon, of course, was the perfect host, sitting at the other end of the table between Sue and Julia and making sure that everyone's glasses were kept filled. The boeuf en croûte was exactly right when Simon carved it, and Cassie was able to give an inaudible sigh of relief and really sit back and enjoy her guests' company, the last small nerve of tension relaxing, knowing now that nothing could go wrong. Not that this was what she thought of as a business dinner party, when they entertained the directors of Simon's firm, for example; no, this was merely for friends who wouldn't mind if the roast was a bit burnt, but even so—perhaps more so— Cassie had tried hard to make everything perfect.

She sat back in her chair and looked at Simon, whose dark head was turned away as he spoke to Sue. Then, almost as if she had spoken his name aloud, he glanced up and caught her eye. He grinned, guessing her thoughts, and lifted his glass in a silent toast of congratulation. Even as he did so the phone rang and he laughed at the way she wrinkled up her nose in vexation before he excused himself and went to answer it on the extension in the bedroom.

He was gone for several minutes and Cassie raised her eyebrows questioningly when he came back, hoping that this wasn't another emergency, but he gave a slight shake of his head and she was able to relax and turn back to talk to John again.

It was late before anyone made a move to leave, after one in the morning, and Cassie was heartily grateful that tomorrow was Saturday and she wouldn't have to work. She felt comfortably warm and lazy from all the wine and good food. They stood at the door, Cassie kissing everyone goodbye and Simon kissing the girls and shaking hands with John and Chris as their guests reiterated their thanks. Then the door was closed and Cassie could yawn luxuriously, able now to show her tiredness.

'That went off very well, I think.' Simon put the chain on the door and walked into the living-room behind her.

'Mm.' Desultorily Cassie began to collect up glasses.

'Leave that till the morning.'

'It won't take long.'

He came up behind her and put his hands on her shoulders. 'You heard me—leave it till tomorrow.'

She recognised the note in his voice immediately and smiled a little as she put down the glasses and let him gently massage her shoulders.

'Mm, that's nice.'

He continued for a few minutes, his long fingers expertly relaxing her, making her feel soft and languorous, but then he stopped and gently pushing aside the curtain of her hair, bent and kissed her neck, travelling upwards to bite the lobe of her ear. Cassie leaned back against him, eyes closed, lips parted as she sighed with pleasure.

'I think you wore that dress on purpose,' Simon murmured into her ear, his breath warm against her skin. 'You know it turns me on.'

She laughed softly. 'But, Simon, *most* of my dresses seem to turn you on.'

'Mm.' His lips explored the long, graceful curve of her neck and his hands had found her breasts. 'And your tight jeans, and bikinis, and those see-through nightdresses you wear to tantalise me.'

Cassie turned to face him and put her arms round his neck. 'That seems to be everything I possess.

'Maybe it's just because you're in them, then.'

He lowered his head to kiss her and Cassie felt the familiar flame of sexuality begin to burn in her veins. Her lips parted under his as she returned his kiss ardently, eagerly. Simon's arms tightened and he pulled her close against him, put a hand low on her

hips, his breathing quickening when she moved voluptuously.

His voice thick, he said, 'Let's go to bed.'

But Cassie decided to tease him a little. 'But the
glasses . . .'

'To hell with the glasses!' He went to draw her towards the bedroom, but she pulled away.

'No, Simon, I really ought to rinse them now.'

His eyes narrowed, but a second later he realised she
was just playing a game and a devilish glint came into
his dark eyes. 'Well, if you won't go to bed . . .' And
he bore her down on to the deep softness of the carpet.

'Simon!' Cassie pretended to be shocked, but her
whole body surged with excitement and anticipation.
It was always like this, had been from the very start;
he had only to kiss her and she wanted him, wanted to
touch and be touched, to love and be loved, to lose
herself in passionate abandon until they reached a
dizzying climax of mutual ecstasy.

He tossed his jacket and tie on to the settee and lay
down beside her, kissing her unhurriedly, but his
hands and lips swiftly rousing her to passion as he
murmured endearments in her ear. He always said the
most wonderful things when he made love, his words
exciting her almost as much as the things he did to
her. She moaned as he fondled her, luxuriating in his
lovemaking, but, as always the first time, impatient to
be taken, wanting him now, now!

But tonight they were interrupted by the insistent
bleep of the telephone, and Cassie groaned as he rolled
off her.

'Damn that thing!' Simon swore as he sat up.

'Don't answer it,' Cassie pleaded, but Simon shook
his head.

'Can't be done, love, I'm afraid. They know I'm here.'

He got up and crossed to lift the receiver, standing with his back to her while he talked. Cassie pulled herself up on to her knees and leant against the settee, straightening her hair and pushing it back over her shoulders while she listened to his end of the conversation. From the sound of it, there was another emergency in Scotland.

Simon confirmed her guess as soon as he replaced the receiver. 'It's the oil terminal again, I'm afraid. And this time the trouble can't be solved over the phone; I'll have to go up there.'

'Oh, Simon, do you have to?'

' 'Fraid so, love.'

Resignedly Cassie went to stand up. 'I'll get your panic bag for you, then, while you change. Are you going by train?'

'No, in the company plane. They're sending a car to pick me up.' He put his hand on her shoulder to stop her rising. 'I told them to get here in half an hour. A lot can happen in half an hour,' he added with a wicked grin as he dropped to his knees beside her.

'Can it?' Cassie smiled back at him and put her hands on his shoulders. 'Such as?'

'Such as this, for a start.' And he again bore her down to the floor.

Simon was ready when the car arrived, but only just; he had only finished dressing as the chauffeur rang the bell. Cassie handed him his overcoat and held his 'panic bag'—a fold-over wardrobe case containing another suit and enough clothes for a two or three-day stay and which was always kept in readiness—while he shrugged it on. Then he grabbed his briefcase and was moving towards the door.

'How long do you think you'll be away?' she asked.

He shrugged. 'No idea. Depends on how much co-operation I get.'

'Mother's invited us to dinner on Daddy's birthday.'

'I should be back easily by then, but I'll phone you anyway.' He put up a hand to push a stray lock of hair from her forehead. Her face was flushed, her long hair dishevelled, and there was a languorous, satiated look about her eyes and mouth. 'You *look* as if you've been made love to,' he told her softly.

Cassie smiled and turned her head to kiss his palm. 'Do I? How do I look?'

'Like a smug, contented cat who's had a saucerful of cream,' he teased her.

She wrinkled her nose. 'I don't think I like that.'

Simon grinned. 'Didn't you? I liked it very much.'

Balling her fist, Cassie gave him a mock thump on the chest. 'That *isn't* what I meant.' But then she was in his arms and he was holding her close. 'Hurry back.'

He kissed her hard once, then more lightly. 'Dream about me.' Then he let her go as he opened the door. 'Don't forget to put the chain on again. 'Bye, darling.'

She heard him greet the chauffeur, and then the door closed and he was gone.

Slowly Cassie put on the chain and turned back into the flat. Suddenly it seemed very empty and very silent. She had been taken to the heights of passion and then back to reality, and the transition had been too fast; she felt empty now and strangely lonely. But then she determinedly shrugged off the feeling and went into the sitting-room to pick up their scattered clothes. She had been left alone in the flat while Simon was away too often to feel alone or afraid now. She put the clothes away and looked rather longingly at the bed, but first went into the kitchen to finish putting the dirty glasses in the dishwasher and turn it on. She shivered and pulled the bathrobe she was wearing tighter round her; it was chilly now that the central heating had turned itself off. Tiredly she went round turning off lights, and got ready for bed, pulling the duvet close around her shoulders. Half asleep, she turned on her side and stretched an arm across to the other side of the big bed, then remembered that Simon wasn't there and curled herself up into a tight ball to fall immediately asleep.

As a fashion buyer, Cassandra only worked from Monday to Friday, but whenever she got the chance she would wander round other department stores to see what the opposition were displaying, so when Julia phoned her late the next morning to thank her for dinner, Cassie suggested that she might like to join her for a couple of hours of window-shopping that afternoon.

'Yes, I'd love to,' Julia agreed. 'I'm a golfing widow today again; John's playing in some tournament or other. Only for heaven's sake don't let me buy anything; John's threatened to divorce me if I do!'

Cassie smiled at Julia's mournful tone. 'Why? Have you been overspending lately?'

'So I've been informed, in no uncertain terms. The trouble is I just can't resist buying something I really like. I bought the most gorgeous evening dress in a little shop in Regent Street last week and it was a bit pricey, I must admit. Those little shops never put a price on the things in their windows, then always charge the earth when you've tried something on and they know you've fallen in love with it. And heaven knows when I'll wear it, because John never takes me out anywhere decent anyway.'

'Well, you'll have to take him out instead,' Cassie replied half flippantly. 'Look, I'll have to go now. I'll meet you at Oxford Circus station at two, okay?'

'Fine. See you.'

It was a good time to go window-shopping; the January sales were over and the fashion departments were full of new stock. Cassie browsed round happily for a couple of hours, making notes on anything that interested her, while Julia was unable to resist buying a skirt and blouse, but Cassie firmly stopped her from buying a pair of shoes and a bag to go with the outfit.

'You've got loads of shoes, Julia, surely you've got a pair you can wear with them?'

'But none that are exactly this tone of beige.'

'Well, wear a contrast colour, then. Your snakeskin shoes would look perfect, much better than an exact match.'

'D'you think so?' Julia held the skirt and shoes together musingly. 'Maybe you're right.' Reluctantly she replaced the shoes on the stand.

'I know I'm right, I'm not a fashion buyer for nothing. Come on, these crowds are getting too much. Let's find somewhere to have a coffee.'

The two girls took the escalator down to the basement and found themselves a table in the coffee shop, which was all apple green walls, white trelliswork decoration and potted plants.

'Ooh, that's better!' Julia gave a sigh of relief as she eased her shoes off under the table. 'Why is it that the pavements around Oxford Street are always harder than anywhere else?'

'You shouldn't wear such high heels,' Cassie told her, without sympathy. 'Are you going to tell John about the things you've bought?'

'No. He won't find out until the credit card statement comes in, and by then we might be on better terms.'

Cassie didn't say anything, letting her friend decide whether or not to take that last remark farther. Julia was silent for a moment, broodingly stirring her coffee, then she burst out, 'Honestly, Cass, you'd never think that John was only a few years older than Simon! Simon still makes a fuss of you and takes you out a lot, whereas all John wants to do when he comes home from work is eat a meal and then collapse in front of the television. *And* he usually falls asleep in the chair!' she added feelingly.

'But don't forget that Simon and I have only been married three years, whereas you've been married ten. Maybe when we've been married that long all Simon will want to do is watch television. Maybe it happens to all men in time.'

Julia's eyebrows rose in disbelief and she shook her head. 'Oh, no. Do you really believe that Simon's the type of man who goes to bed and then tells his wife that *he's* too tired to make love?'

Cassie had to laugh at Julia's outraged face. 'Oh, come on, it's not as bad as that, surely?'

'Near enough. If I didn't know that John was just too lazy, I'd say that he was having an affair.'

'Oh, you don't really think that, Julia? You can't!' There was real shock in Cassie's voice. 'Why, John dotes on you and the children.'

Julia sighed. 'Yes, I know he does. And I'm sure he's faithful. It's just that . . .' She shrugged rather helplessly. 'It's just that I wish he was more *alive*, younger in spirit. Sometimes he seems about sixty years old, when he's not even forty yet.'

Cassie thought it wiser to change the subject then, and they talked of other things until Julia mentioned the dinner party the previous night.

'They were a nice couple, Sue and Christopher. Have you known them long?'

'No, only a few months. Sue only came to work at Marriott & Brown's after they got married.'

'They haven't been married very long, then?'

'No, just over a year, I think.'

'He seemed interesting; quite a sporty type by the look of him.'

There was something in Julia's voice that made Cassie look at her quickly, but the elder girl's face was quite impassive, her attention given to the cream cake she was cutting.

'Yes, I believe he's a squash addict.'

'They usually are nowadays; no one seems to go in for tennis any more. It's either squash or badminton. Oh, by the way,' Julia licked cream off her lips, 'perhaps you could give me Sue's telephone number. I promised to give her my recipe for salmon mousse, but she forgot to give me her number.'

'I'll write it down for you.' Cassie jotted the number on a page torn out of her notebook and passed it over, looking at her friend searchingly, but Julia was completely casual as she took it and dropped it in her bag. Cassie chided herself for being a fool; as if Julia would be interested in a boy six years younger than herself!

They parted soon after and Cassie went home to

spend the rest of the weekend catching up on jobs. Simon phoned every evening, but it seemed that the labour problems were even worse than he had feared, and they were also having trouble from a group of environmentalists who were trying to disrupt the building of the new terminal.

Monday was a busy day: getting the computer readings of all the stock sold during the last week, re-ordering where necessary, interviewing sales reps, looking at samples, writing to the firms whose garments she had admired in other shops and asking for catalogues and quotes. She was constantly being sought out to make decisions all day. She was busy, but she carried out all her tasks efficiently and in a businesslike manner, not asking for anyone's advice and not afraid of making her own decisions. The job was demanding and required her constant attention and energy. But Cassie loved it, loved the adrenalin it roused, the excitement of choosing from the new collections and the satisfaction when a line sold particularly well, especially when it was a Marriott & Brown's exclusive. She had come a long way in the five years she had been working there, first as a humble trainee, then working her way up to be an assistant to a very small department, then a larger one, and eventually to have a department of her own. Her flair for clothes had certainly helped her, but she also had an instinctive idea of what women, the younger generation especially, wanted. She seemed to have a constant finger on the pulse of fashion and could tell what London girls would be wearing six months before they even thought of buying. So now she controlled all the buying for the 'Top Togs' department which filled half the basement of Marriott & Brown's.

The rest of the week fell into the same busy pattern, except that at the weekly buyers' conference on Thursday she was asked to go to Paris on the following Monday to select some goods from the new designer collections which would eventually go on sale in the shop in the autumn. Cassie accepted eagerly; this was quite a feather in her cap as she hadn't yet been entrusted with many buying trips abroad and had always before gone in company with another more experienced buyer, but this time she was to go alone because the head buyer for the fashion department was away on a skiing holiday. Cassie was very pleased, because she by no means intended to remain as she was; her ambition was to eventually become the head buyer for the whole of the fashion department, and even that wouldn't be the end; there were far bigger organisations than Marriott & Brown's in the fashion world.

It was her father's birthday on Sunday and Cassie was beginning to be afraid that Simon wouldn't be able to make it. Although he hadn't gone into details over the phone, she had gathered that the problems at the terminal were tougher than he had anticipated and consequently would take longer to solve. But he assured her that he would do everything he could to make it, and with that she had to be content. Not that Cassie was the one who was really worried about him not being there; it was her mother who always liked to have the entire family gathered around her on such occasions, and that included son and daughters-in-law as well as Cassie and her two brothers. Also she knew that her father had a special regard for Simon and would be disappointed if he couldn't make it, even though he wouldn't say anything or show it.

By Sunday morning she had resigned herself to

having to go alone, but at eleven o'clock when she was having a long soak in the bath, the radio playing the latest hit tunes nearby and a book in her hands, the door was pushed open and Simon walked in. The noise from the radio had drowned the sounds of his arrival, and she jumped with fright when he suddenly appeared.

He grinned at the consternation on her face. 'It's all right, it's only me.'

'God, what a fright you gave me! Oh, lor', you made me drop my book in the water, and it's a library book too!' She fished in the bubbly water and brought out the sopping book. 'Now I suppose I'll have to pay for it.'

'See what it's like when it dries out.' Firmly Simon took the book from her and put it to one side. 'Now, woman, I've been away for a whole week. How about greeting me properly?'

He knelt down beside the bath and Cassie tilted her head up to kiss him. His lips held hers for a long time, gradually becoming harder, and his voice was thick when at last he drew away and said, 'Wouldn't you like your back scrubbed?'

'All right.'

She found the soap and gave it to him and then slowly stood up. The water ran in rivulets down her slender body, but here and there the bubbles still clung as if reluctant to leave her. Her long chestnut hair she had piled on top of her head, but a few tendrils hung damply on her neck. She turned her back on Simon and he carefully moved aside the clinging strands of hair before he began to soap her. His hands moved in unison over her, starting at her shoulders and moving slowly down to her hips, his fingers firm and caressing.

'Turn around,' he demanded after a while, his voice husky.

Slowly she did so, her tongue licking lips gone suddenly dry, her body starting to tremble in anticipation. It was strange to be in the bathroom together like this, Simon fully dressed and she stark naked. He resoaped his hands and they began to slide over her, the soap leaving long white finger strokes as his hands gently circled each curve, aroused every sexual nerve end. Excitement surged through her and Cassie gasped as he found and fondled a particularly sensitive place. Her breasts hardened and she pushed herself against his hands, eyes half closed with desire, her breath panting through lips drawn back in ecstasy.

Suddenly Simon made a sort of groaning sound deep in his throat and he lifted her bodily out of the bath, still wet and soapy as she was, and carried her into the bedroom. He kissed her as he carried her and kept on kissing her as he laid her down on the bed and stripped off his clothes. The first time he made love to her hungrily, urgently, as if he'd been away much longer than just a week, but the second time he did so slowly, pleasurably, taking delight in her body until he was again consumed by thrusting passion.

Later, in the early evening, they drove out of London to Cassie's parents' home in Buckinghamshire, and she took the opportunity to tell Simon about her trip to Paris the following day.

'It isn't one of the big fashion house collections, of course, otherwise they would have sent one of the senior buyers instead of me, but it's by a comparatively new group of designers who've got together and produced a whole range of clothes for young girls—the teens and twenties age range mostly. They sound really exciting, just the thing we need to lift Top Togs into being the most up-to-date department in London,' she told him enthusiastically.

'When exactly are you leaving?'

'Early tomorrow morning. I have to be at Heathrow by eight-thirty.'

Simon's dark brows drew into a slight frown. 'Then we only have tonight.'

Cassie smiled and leaned against his shoulder. 'But we had this afternoon,' she reminded him gently.

'So we did.' His hand came down to cover hers for a moment, but then he had to put it back on the steering wheel as he overtook a slow-moving lorry. 'I'm afraid I won't be able to drive you to the airport, darling; I have to be at the office at nine to attend a meeting to try and find a solution to the oil terminal crisis.'

'Crisis? That's rather a strong word. Is it really as bad as that?'

Simon nodded grimly. 'It's certainly getting that way. The man in overall charge of the project doesn't seem to be able to cope. Or maybe it's because he's resentful because his company was taken over by Mullaine's and he isn't trying. I certainly didn't get much in the way of co-operation from him.'

'Does that mean you'll have to go up there again?'

'Very likely. I can't see it getting sorted out unless I do.'

Cassie wrinkled her nose in sympathy. 'That's a shame. The terminal's miles from anywhere, isn't it? You must be bored out of your mind in the evenings.'

'Too many worries on my plate to be bored. But it is a lonely place. There was nothing but sheep and seabirds before they decided to build the oil terminal there.'

'Didn't the local people object?'

'Yes, but it was an area of massive unemployment, so they really had no choice but to agree. Better to lose one bay on the coast than to have several thousand people on the dole.'

Shortly afterwards they arrived at the house and were immediately caught up in purely family matters: congratulating her father, greeting the rest of the family and swapping gossip with her two brothers and their wives. After the meal Cassie helped her mother to wash up; the other girls had also offered to help, but her mother had insisted that they stay in the living-room with the men, saying that she and Cassie could manage. For some time they made small talk about everyday matters, but Cassie knew that her mother was working up to the subject she always brought up whenever she could get her daughter alone. Naughtily Cassie, half teasing, half serious, put her off by quickly opening up a new topic every time there was a pause and her mother opened her mouth to speak. But at last, exasperated, the older woman said bluntly, 'I suppose you haven't decided to start a family yet?'

'No, Mother,' Cassie agreed. 'You're right, we haven't.'

'Well, I don't know why not. You're nearly twenty-five; it's high time you had a baby. I'm sure Simon would love to have children, and he'd make a very good father.'

'Whenever he happened to be home to see them, you mean.' Cassie commented drily. Then, impatiently, 'I've told you dozens of times, Mother, we don't want any children, we're perfectly happy as we are.'

'Oh, really!' Her mother banged a saucepan down

angrily on to the draining-board. 'I don't know what your generation think you're doing. Three children all married and not one of you with any babies. What's the point of getting married at all if you're not going to have any children?'

'Are you suggesting that you would prefer us to be living in sin?' Cassie demanded tartly.

'Certainly not! You know full well what I mean.' Seeing that she wasn't getting anywhere, the older woman changed tactics. 'Your father isn't getting any younger, you know. He was saying only today how much he'd love to have a grandchild before he gets too old.'

'Oh, Mother,' Cassie exclaimed exasperatedly, 'he's not even sixty yet. Anyone would think he'd got one foot in the grave, to listen to you.'

'Well, he probably will have if he waits for you. And anyway, he'll be retiring soon,' her mother added defensively. 'It would be nice to have grandchildren we could take on outings.'

'Well, go and talk to your daughters-in-law, then,' Cassie told her without sympathy, 'because I certainly don't intend to saddle myself with children just to satisfy your grandmaternal instincts.'

'You know I can't talk to them about it. They don't like it if I do.'

'No, and nor do I.' Cassie dropped the tea-towel on to the draining-board. 'We live in an entirely different world from the one when you were a young wife. We can choose our own way of life and whether or not to have a career. Motherhood isn't the be-all and end-all that it was when you got married, Mother, and frankly, quite apart from the fact that they would be an unwanted encumbrance, the whole idea of having children bores me to tears!' Then Cassie turned on her heel and walked firmly out of the kitchen, two bright patches of angry colour on her cheeks.

Everyone looked at her curiously as she entered the sitting-room and she realised with some annoyance that they must have heard the raised voices. No one said anything, though, and the episode was glossed over, although her mother rather pointedly ignored her for an hour or so afterwards.

On the way home Simon asked her, 'What was all that about?'

Cassie shrugged. 'Oh, the usual thing: when are we going to start a family. Though why she always picks on me when the others have been married longer, I don't know.'

'What did you tell her?'

'That we didn't want any children, of course, ever. We agreed on that right at the start.'

'Did we? I don't remember incorporating it into the marriage vows.'

The slightly sardonic note in his voice made Cassie look at him sharply, but then she laughed. 'Simon, don't tease. You know it was an accepted thing.'

He was silent for a moment, then said rather absently, 'Yes, of course.'

He changed the subject then, and it seemed no time at all before they got home, grabbed a few hours' sleep and Cassie was rushing around to get ready for the trip to Paris. Simon dropped her off at the Underground station and Cassie gave him a swift kiss of farewell.

' 'Bye, darling. Must rush—I'm sure I'm going to be late,' Cassie said hurriedly as she hauled her case out of the car.

Simon laughed. 'Stop panicking, you've got plenty of time.'

But Cassie was already shutting the car door. 'I'll call you tonight. 'Bye!'

But when she did finally get round to phoning him late that evening her only reply was from the metallic-sounding voice on the answer-phone tape. She had spent an exciting, exhausting day booking into a hotel, meeting her French contacts, and being introduced to the team of young French designers, who had insisted on taking her out to dinner. Cassie spoke French reasonably well, but it had been a strain trying to follow and join in a conversation on style and design that had turned into a prolonged debate with good-natured but voluble argument ranging back and forth, and it had been late when they finally broke up and she had got a taxi back to her hotel.

Now she looked down at the receiver in her hand in some puzzlement, almost as if it could tell her why her husband didn't answer. Her finely-arched brows drew together into a frown, then she shrugged philosophically. Well, there was nothing she could do about it here and now anyway. Stifling a yawn, she left a message for him on the tape to say that she had arrived safely, then got ready for bed. This kind of life was very stimulating, of course, but it was also certainly very tiring.

The next two days were also extremely hectic as Cassie attended the fashion show, taking notes of the garments she particularly liked the look of, and got together with the designers and a French manufacturer who was to produce cheaper versions of the clothes for Marriott & Brown's. Quite a lot of haggling took place and, being in France, most of it was done over a meal and a bottle of wine. There was also a trip out to a fabrics factory so that Cassie could check on the quality of the cloth that was to be used, and here again there was some hard bargaining, but at last they managed to agree on figures for quantity and price that left everyone happy, and Cassie also had the satisfaction of getting the designers to sign an exclusive contract with Marriott & Brown's which also gave them the first refusal on their next season's collection.

Somehow, during that second busy day, she found the time to phone Simon's office and they told her that he had gone back to Scotland, which she had already guessed was the most probable reason for his absence. They gave her a number to ring and she tried it that evening, but she had such a terrible time trying to get through that in the end she just gave it up as a bad job.

Thursday saw her back in London, but when she took the lift up to the top floor of the Marriott & Brown building to her office to make out her report on the Paris trip, she was immediately greeted by the news that Don Ashby, the head buyer for the whole of the fashion department, had broken a leg while skiing and wouldn't be able to return to work for quite some time.

'We only heard yesterday,' her secretary told her excitedly. 'It seems he went out on the ski slopes after a blizzard during the night, but there was ice under the snow and he lost control. Fractured his leg in two places, he did. Not just broke it, but *fractured* it,' the girl added with morbid enjoyment. 'Oh, and Mr Jepps said I was to ask you to go to his office as soon as you arrived.'

Cassie thanked her rather faintly and made her way to the office of the Buying Manager, thinking that if her own plane had crashed on the way back from Paris it would really have made her secretary's day! She didn't have to wait long in the outer office before she was told to go in to see Mr Jepps, who was the head of the Buying Department and also a director of the firm.

After exchanging greetings, she started to tell him about her trip to Paris, but he stopped her almost at once.

'Tell me about that later. Have you heard about poor Ashby?'

'Yes, my secretary just told me. Is he really that badly hurt, or has it gained in the telling?'

'That bad, I'm afraid. He's going to be out of commission for at least six months. So I've decided to rearrange the buying responsibilities for the fashion department. I'm putting Mrs Nichols in general charge and I want you to take over all her departments as well as your own. Can you do that?'

He looked at her keenly, but for a moment Cassie could only stare at him open-mouthed. Then she hastily pulled herself together and said, 'Yes. Yes, I know I can. Thank you for—for giving me the chance.'

He smiled. 'Well, you'd better cut along and talk to Mrs Nichols as soon as you can. You can tell me all about the Paris trip some other time. Oh, and by the way,' he added as she moved towards the door, 'there will, of course, be a raise in salary and expense allowance while you have the extra responsibility.'

Simon arrived home again on Friday, going first to the office to discuss the oil terminal problems with the directors. He looked tired and there was a taut, strained look about his eyes when he came into the flat, but Cassie was keyed up with excitement; she seemed to have been on a high ever since she'd heard of her temporary promotion, and hadn't yet come back down to earth. She was full of ideas that would give the various departments now under her control a more modern image and was wild to tell Simon about them and use him as a sounding board, but she held herself in check until he'd changed and waited until they were seated at a table in their favourite bistro-type restaurant before she told him.

'Oh, don't bother with that, let's just have the usual wine.' Impatiently she took the wine list he had been about to study and gave it back to the waiter. 'I've got something to tell you.'

Simon smiled slightly and nodded to the waiter. 'The Mosel, please.' Then he turned to her, the smile deepening. 'All right, what is it? Something pretty good, from the look of you. Did the Paris trip go well?'

'What? Oh, yes, fine.' Cassie dismissed Paris with a wave of her hand. 'This is much more important news. You know Don Ashby, the head fashion buyer? Well, he's broken his leg.'

Simon's left eyebrow rose. 'That's supposed to be good news?'

'Not for poor old Don, of course, but it is for me.' She raised a glowing face to his. 'Mrs Nichols has taken over Don's work and . . .' she paused, her eyes bright with excitement, 'oh, Simon, I've been put in charge of all Mrs Nichols's departments! That's the designer rooms, evening and day dresses, separates and swimwear, as well as Top Togs.'

Simon stared at her for a long moment before saying slowly, 'I see.'

'But do you?' Cassie demanded, impatient at his apparent lack of interest, wanting him to share her excitement. 'Can't you see it's my chance to really prove myself? Top Togs has been a great success, but it was an entirely new innovation. The store had had nothing like it before and so they've been unable to compare my work with anything else. For all they know anyone could have done it. But now that I've got all those departments that have been in the store from the beginning I'll be able to show the directors how sales can be improved by a really modern approach. Fashionwise those departments are still back in the Middle-Ages.'

She paused as the waiter brought their first course and poured the wine, looking at Simon with a puzzled frown. He didn't seem to be sharing her excitement at all, in fact he had a rather frowning look in his dark eyes. Which was unusual for him, usually he was right in there, encouraging her, listening to her problems, giving advice and help. But tonight he seemed to have something on his mind and didn't even look pleased to hear her news.

'Well,' she demanded as soon as the waiter had gone, 'don't you think it's the most marvellous chance? If I make a really big success of it I might even be allowed to keep the departments, because Mrs Nichols is due to retire in a couple of years.'

'And what does Mrs Nichols do in the meantime?' Simon asked drily.

Cassie shrugged irritably. 'Oh, I don't know. They'll find her something, they always do. Well,' she demanded again, 'what do you think?'

'It's a wonderful opportunity, of course. But,' a rueful look came into his eyes, 'as a matter of fact I have some news of my own. At the Directors' meeting I went to today it was decided to get rid of the chap who's been in charge of the oil terminal up to now and put a new man in his place. And the man would have to be at director level to have the necessary authority to take over.' He picked up his glass and took a drink, then set it down, his eyes fixed on hers. 'And they've offered me the job with a junior directorship.'

'A directorship?' Cassie's eyes lit up with surprise and pleasure. 'Why, Simon, that's marvellous!'

She went to go on, but Simon stopped her. 'Is it?'

'Why, what do you mean?'

Deliberately he replied, 'To get the directorship I have to take the job—and the job means that we'll have to leave London at once and go to live in Scotland for at least three years!'

CHAPTER TWO

FOR a full minute Cassie could only stare at him in dumbfounded amazement. Then, her voice sticking in her throat, she stuttered, 'Scotland? For three years? It's a joke, yes? Please tell me it's a joke,' she added, watching him hopefully, but he didn't answer, just sat looking at her with the same half rueful, half troubled expression. Slowly she sat back with a sigh and put down her fork. 'You're not joking.'

'Afraid not, darling.'

Cassie shrugged. 'Oh, well, the idea was nice while it lasted. Never mind, darling, I expect something else will come along some time soon.'

Simon's eyes narrowed slightly. 'For whom?'

Eyebrows rising in surprise, Cassie replied, 'For you, of course. Mullaine's are bound to offer you another directorship sooner or later.'

'Not necessarily. Vacancies for junior directors aren't that thick on the ground. If I turn this one down for no reason they're going to think twice before offering me another.'

'But you've got a reason,' Cassie pointed out. 'It's in Scotland. No one in their right mind is going to bury themselves alive in Scotland for three years!'

'Except the few million Scots who happen to live there,' Simon put in sardonically.

'Unfortunately the poor things are stuck with it. But that's neither here nor there.' Cassie dismissed the entire Scottish population with a shrug of her shoulders. 'Simon, you can't even contemplate going there. Why, the place is dead, a cultural desert. It's all snow, football hooligans, and those dreadful accents that you can't understand a word of. And didn't you say that the oil terminal is on the coast, absolutely miles from anywhere?'

'It is in a remote spot, yes. It has to be, for fear of an accident, but . . .'

'You mean it's likely to blow up at any moment?' Cassie interrupted caustically. 'Charming!'

Simon's features hardened, his lips drawing into a thin line. 'That's always a possibility that has to be taken into account when any kind of fuel is being stored. But the site director's house is over a mile from the terminal, you can't even see it. It sits by itself in the next valley with beautiful views over the sea.'

Cassie's green eyes widened as she stared at him. 'The site director's house? You mean you've already been to see it? Simon, you're not—surely you're not seriously considering this crazy idea?'

Tight-lipped, her husband said firmly, 'Yes, I am.'

'But—but you can't! What about my job, my promotion?' Simon's lips twisted into a grimace and he opened his mouth to speak, but before he could do so Cassie added in obstinate anger, 'I'm not going to give it up, Simon. I'm just not!'

His dark brows drew into a sharp frown as he said shortly, 'Well, thanks for all the loving co-operation and understanding.'

Cassie bit her lip, but had to stay silent while the waiter came to take away their plates and bring the second course. She looked at the succulent food on her plate and found that her appetite had completely gone; she wished that she'd never ordered it, wished that they were at home.

As soon as the man had gone she tried to placate Simon by saying, 'Look, I'm sorry if I was a bit blunt, but my . . .'

'Leave it,' he commanded brusquely. 'We'll discuss it when we get home.'

But his high-handed tone annoyed her. 'No, I won't leave it. It concerns me as much as it does you. My job's important to me, Simon, and I don't think you have any right to ask me to give it up.'

'And has it occurred to you that my job is of equal, if not more importance, to me?'

'I don't see how it can be more important.'

'Possibly because I'm supposed to be the bread-winner,' Simon pointed out in heavy sarcasm.

'Oh, rubbish! That kind of thinking went out with the Ark. Marriage is an equal partnership now, and I have a right to work if I want to. And anyway, we need the money that I earn.'

Anger came into Simon's eyes as he leaned towards her and said forcefully. 'You know darn well that isn't true. I was earning quite enough to support you when we married, but you *wanted* to go on working, no one was forcing you to, so don't try and make out that we'd be on the breadline without your salary.'

Cassie's mouth set into a petulant line. 'Oh, I see, so now my salary is of no importance.'

'I didn't say that,' Simon returned exasperatedly. 'Of course your money is extremely useful. I was only saying that you don't *have* to work.'

Moodily Cassie glared down at her plate and picked at the food on it. She had been so looking forward to tonight and now the whole evening was ruined. Simon, too, attacked his meal, pleased to let the matter drop for the time being, but Cassie couldn't let it alone. 'Okay,' she said after a minute or two, 'maybe I don't have to work from the financial point of view, but I do need to work for creative satisfaction. I'm not one of those women who could sit at home all day with nothing to do. You know I'm not.'

'Other women seem to find plenty to fill their time,' Simon pointed out reasonably.

'Oh, coffee mornings and afternoon bridge parties. That's not being creative. And anyway, women like that develop into neurotics who live on Valium pills after a few years. Either that, or they feel that they have to start having children to justify their existence. And that's in London where you have cinemas, theatres, museums and galleries to go to. Heaven alone knows what it would be like in Scotland. I'd probably go stark, staring mad within three months,' she added morosely.

'It isn't the back of beyond,' Simon told her impatiently. 'A daily shuttle plane flies from Glasgow to London. If you did feel that you were incapable of sustaining life with only me for company, you could always catch it and come to town for a few days.'

Cassie looked across at him quickly, the note of acerbity in his voice surprising her because it wasn't one she was used to hearing directed at her, but before she could make any remark, Simon pushed his hardly-touched plate away and said, 'I don't want this. How about you?'

'No.'

'Let's get out of here, then.'

He called the waiter over and asked for the bill, but had to give repeated assurances that there was nothing wrong with the food before he was allowed to produce his Diners Card and pay.

On the short drive home Cassie was silent, trying to work out all the arguments she could use to try and make Simon change his mind. Not that she didn't sympathise with him; to have been offered a director-ship in such a large and important company as Mullaine's at the relatively early age of thirty-two was, she knew, a real advancement and proved that they had great faith in him. But to go to live in Scotland—it just wasn't on.

Back in the flat, Simon immediately walked over to the drinks cabinet and poured himself a large whisky.

'I'd like one too,' Cassie told him tartly, although she hadn't wanted a drink until she saw that he hadn't bothered to get her one.

'Sorry.' He handed her a glass and then went to sit on the settee. Cassie sat opposite him in the armchair and took a rather defiant drink of whisky.

'Look, darling, I'm sorry if this means that you'll lose your chance of being a director for a while, but I just couldn't live in Scotland, I *know* I couldn't. I'd never be happy there.' She looked at him pleadingly. 'Please try to understand, Simon.'

'Oh, I understand all right,' he answered bitterly. 'You want everything to go your way and you aren't willing to make any sacrifices, or even any concessions, to please someone else.'

Cassie fired up immediately. 'Why should *I* be the one to make concessions and sacrifices? I've just reached the highest I've ever got in my job and you're asking me to give it up.'

Simon drained off his whisky and stood up. 'So are you,' he pointed out heavily. 'And don't forget that I've worked just as damned hard, and for longer, to get where I am. But that seems to mean nothing to you; without much thought—and certainly without a qualm—you expect—no, demand, that I should give up what is virtually an unprecedented rise to director level. The fact that I'll then lose the confidence and reliance that the Board of Directors have placed in me seems to be completely immaterial to you.

'For God's sake use your brain and think, Cassie. Or even bring it down to the basis of economics; whether you like it or not, I'm earning more money than you and therefore my job is more important to us.'

'But mine has great potential,' Cassie put in heatedly.

Simon's face hardened, grew grim. 'So has mine—and for a while today I had the laughable belief that you would be pleased that I'd achieved that potential—not throw it back in my face!' He shot the last sentence at her, waited for her to reply, but when she didn't turned on his heel and walked out of the room towards the hall.

Cassie gaped in surprise for a moment and then got up to run after him. 'Where are you going?'

'Down to the pub for a drink.'

'Don't you dare walk out on me when we're in the middle of a discussion!'

'Is that what you call it?' he demanded jeeringly.

'All right, argument, then.'

He turned on her, suddenly angry. 'What's the point of going on? It's checkmate. You won't give up your job and I won't give up mine. So, unless one of us is prepared to give in, we've reached an impasse. And as I don't feel like arguing round and round the subject all evening, I'm going out for an hour.'

'Just an hour?' Her voice was small, uncertain.

'Just an hour,' he agreed, and Cassie was relieved to hear some of the coldness had gone from his voice.

She was sitting on the settee watching television when he got back, but her attention hadn't really been on the screen, she'd been thinking about the situation and realised that she wasn't handling it very well. Coming right out and saying that she refused to go to Scotland had put Simon's back up. She was asking him to give up a lot, and there were more persuasive ways for a woman to get what she wanted than having a stand-up fight about it. So she'd changed into a new black lace nightdress that she'd bought in Paris and he hadn't seen before and brushed her hair until it shone like a brilliant flame upon her shoulders.

Simon didn't speak when he came in, just tossed his jacket to one side and came to sit at the other end of the settee, picking up her bare feet to make room and resting them in his lap. Idly he began to play with her toes, and Cassie was glad that she'd painted the nails with a delicate pearly-pink varnish.

'Was there anyone at the pub that we know?' she asked him, liking the way his hands caressed her feet.

'Just a couple of the chaps from the tennis club. They didn't have their wives with them.'

'Oh.' His hands moved down from her toes and tickled so that Cassie wriggled her feet.

'Sorry.'

He went to let go of her feet, but Cassie said swiftly, 'No, I like it. It just tickled, that's all. Don't stop.'

He smiled slightly. 'You'll be telling me next I'm a foot fetishist!'

'I always wondered how people like that get their kicks.'

'With feet as perfect as yours it's hardly surprising.' And lifting up her foot he kissed her instep.

'Hmm. Of course, you don't find any women who're foot fetishists.'

Simon burst out laughing. 'Are you saying that all men have ugly feet? You're crazy, you know that.' He looked at her then stretched out a hand. 'Come here, woman.'

Happily Cassie twisted round until she was sitting on his lap, her arm round his neck.

'Is that a new nightdress?'

'Yes.'

His eyes ran over it, taking in the while gleam of her skin behind the thin lace, the curves of her waist and hips. 'It's very sexy. Why don't you take it off?'

'Simon!'

'Well, that's the idea of sexy nightwear, isn't it? That it's to be taken off?'

'You have no romance in your soul,' Cassie complained. 'A girl likes to be flattered a little first.'

'I've already told you you've got beautiful feet, what more do you want?'

'There's more to me than my feet,' she pointed out.

'Mm, so I've noticed.' Undoing the silk bow at the front of the nightdress, he parted it to reveal the creamy swell of her breasts. He undid another bow to open it to the waist, then his hands moved inside to cup the soft fullness of her breasts, to gently fondle and caress them until they hardened under his hands, thrust towards his mouth as he bent to kiss them.

Cassie put her hand down to hold his head there, loving what he was doing to her, the soft, insistent pull of his lips already driving her wild with desire. His head came up and he kissed her hard on the mouth, bending her head back against the arm of the settee.

'Does this nightdress turn you on?'

Simon laughed softly. 'Now who isn't being romantic?'

'Does it?' she insisted.

'Why don't you find out for yourself?' He took her hand and guided it down.

'Oh, Simon.' Her eyes gazed into his pleadingly. 'I love you so much. Please, please don't let's argue any more. I can't stand it when we fight.'

For a moment his hand tightened on her arm, hurting her so that Cassie bit her lip to stifle a wince of pain, fleetingly afraid that she had been too direct, had aroused his anger again, but then he said roughly, 'Don't worry, we'll work something out. We have to work something out.'

And she knew a glow of inner satisfaction as she passionately returned his kiss, using every sexual wile she knew to rouse him into a violent storm of lovemaking, from which all outside problems and differences were completely obliterated.

It was Saturday the next morning and Cassie slept late, the strident ring of the alarm clock turned off and nothing to disturb her except the usual incessant hum of traffic that was so much part of the background that only its absence would have penetrated. She finally woke about nine, turned over in bed and realised that she was naked. Simon wasn't beside her, so she hurriedly slipped out of bed and pulled on a bathrobe, fully aware that, although their quarrel last night had been more than adequately made up, it still hadn't been settled. She padded out of the bedroom and through the flat, looking for him, her bare toes sinking into the soft, deep pile of the carpet.

He was sitting in an easy chair by the window of the sitting-room, reading the morning paper in the soft February sunlight, casually dressed in jeans and a sweater, an empty cup of coffee on the small table beside him. As she came in he looked up, smiled and held out a hand to her. Cassie went to him at once, took his hand and bent down to kiss him.

When she raised her head he kept hold of her hand as he said, 'You look very sexy like that, still half asleep and your hair tousled. I've a good mind to take you back to bed.'

Cassie laughed at him and backed quickly away. 'Not until I've showered and cleaned my teeth, and then I'll be fully awake and you won't feel like it any more.' She turned to go to the bathroom, but paused in the doorway. 'What are the plans for today? Do you want to go down to the Portobello Road antique market, or would you rather go up to the West End to do some shopping?'

Simon regarded her levelly. 'Maybe we'll go out later on, but right now I think we have some talking to do, don't you?'

The bright smile faded from Cassie's face. 'Can't it wait until some other time? Tomorrow maybe?'

Simon shook his head in a single, curtly negative gesture. 'No, we have to settle it here and now.'

Her voice tight and a little unsteady, Cassie shrugged and said, 'Okay, if that's what you want.'

She had spoken casually enough, but her heart was beating rather fast and she felt strangely nervous as, fully dressed and carrying a mug of coffee, she came to sit down opposite him.

Simon tossed aside the newspaper and ran his eyes over her, taking in her black sweater and long legs in black cord designer jeans. If he also noted the wary look in her eyes that she was trying unsuccessfully to hide, he gave no sign of it. He merely looked amused and said, 'Why the all-black outfit? Do you intend to take up cat-burglary or are you going to a funeral?'

Cassie shrugged rather impatiently. 'I just felt like wearing them, that's all.'

'Because they suit your mood?'

Her eyes flicked over him and then quickly away. Damn Simon; he knew her far too well. 'I'm *not* in a black mood, if that's what you're trying to imply.' She made a business of stirring her coffee. 'All right, you wanted to talk, so why don't you start?'

'All right.' He leant back in the chair and put his hands together, pyramiding his fingers, his face stern and serious, and Cassie had a sudden insight into how he must appear to his colleagues, especially those under him; highly intelligent, coldly efficient and rather remote. For a brief second he seemed to be a stranger and the idea frightened her, but then he spoke again and the feeling was gone. 'Straight question—after sleeping on it are you willing to give up your job and come with me to Scotland?'

'No.'

His dark brows flickered at the boldness of her answer, but he went on, 'Not under any circumstances?'

'None that I can envisage.'

'I see.'

He paused for a moment and Cassie said impatiently, 'Look, Simon, what's the point of this? Nothing's changed since last night. I'm sorry, but I just don't want to go.'

The skin at his fingertips whitened as he pressed

them harder together, but he said easily, 'But let's bear in mind that you haven't even seen Kinray yet.'

'Kinray? Is that where the oil terminal is?'

'Yes. It's on the north-west coast of Scotland and is actually called Mull of Kinray. As I told you, the house is about a mile from the terminal and hidden from it by a range of hills. It faces the Atlantic and has the most marvellous views of the sea and coastline, with the hills, purple with heather in summer, to the right and behind it. The first time I went up I stayed there for a couple of days and it was fascinating to have the whole valley, or glen as they call it, filled with a mist that comes up from the sea in the morning, which would gradually thin and then suddenly lift to reveal this most fantastically beautiful scenery.'

Cassie gazed at him for a long moment, for the second time feeling that she was talking to a stranger, but an entirely different one this time; Simon didn't usually wax eloquent about places he'd visited. And the idea that he had found somewhere beautiful made her feel strangely jealous; *she* wanted to be the only beautiful object in his life. But then she realised that he was trying to sell the place to her and that he was bound to come over strong. So, to squash any hopes he might have on that score, she said sardonically, 'It sounds extremely cold and damp. It must be hell there in the winter, with the gales blowing in straight off the Atlantic. And it must get snowed up all the time—they always have terrific amounts of snow in Scotland.'

Simon looked at her for a moment over his steepled fingers, then lowered them as he said, 'Strangely enough they don't have very extreme weather in that area because it's in the path of the Gulf Stream. You can even grow palm trees and other tropical plants there. That's one of the reasons why the oil terminal was sited in that area.'

'So that they could grow palm trees?' Cassie quipped. 'What are they going to do—resort to palm oil if North Sea oil runs out?'

'Ha, ha. Very funny.' Simon stood up abruptly, anger in his face. 'When you've finished making cheap puns perhaps you'd care to remember that this is our future we're discussing. Perhaps even a future in which we would be able to see more of each other, not just pass one another going through the door and correspond in notes stuck on the fridge door or messages left on the answer-phone,' he added grimly.

Cassie instantly felt ashamed and got up to follow him as he went into the kitchen. Plugging in the percolator, he stood silently waiting for it to heat, his face averted.

After a moment, Cassie said exasperatedly, 'All right, I'm sorry. But let's face it, Simon, all you've done so far is try to sell me something I don't want to buy. Okay, the place may be beautiful on summer days when the mist lifts and the sun shines. But what about all those other days: the days when it rains incessantly or the place is shrouded in cold, damp mist for the whole twenty-four hours? I've been on holiday to Scotland more than once with my parents, Simon, I *know* how miserable the weather can be. And even then there's all the other things that would be missing—work, entertainment, friends.'

The percolator started to bubble and the red light went out. Simon switched it off and picked it up to pour himself another cup of coffee. 'Couldn't you look on it as a sort of sabbatical, an interval of peace and quiet in between work? You could always go back to work afterwards.'

'Simon, it's three years! In that time I'd have lost most of my contacts, someone else would have taken my position and consolidated themselves in it. Fashion buying is just as much a cut-throat business as anything else; if you leave it for any length of time there's little or no chance of getting back. It's all or nothing.'

Simon looked at her keenly, the coffee pot still raised in his hand. 'Will you at least meet me halfway by coming with me to Kinray to see the place before making any final decision?'

Cassie shook her head unhappily. 'Simon, it wouldn't do any good. I've already . . .'

'Will you?' he interrupted her, his voice suddenly harsh and cold.

She stared at him, realising that never before had she ever deliberately defied her husband, that she hardly knew him now that his will was crossed. It was something new and something she didn't know how to handle. There was no other way out, so slowly, almost in a whisper, she answered, 'Yes, all right. If that's what you want.'

'It is.' He set the coffee-pot down with a snap. 'We'll go up there next weekend.'

Her lips drawn into a tight line, Cassie glanced at him for a moment, then said, 'Well, now that's settled, perhaps we can get on with the present. I'll go and get ready to go to the antique market; if you remember we said we'd go and look for that little table we wanted for the hall.'

She turned and went into the bedroom, Simon watching her frowningly. She hadn't openly defied him, of course, but by wanting to go out and choose something for their present home she had clearly shown how little importance she placed on the projected trip to Kinray. It was just going to be a complete waste of time, Cassie thought as she put on her lipstick, watching her image in the mirror. They would have a long, tedious and tiring forty-eight hours in which she would take one look at the place and make the same refusals as she had already made here. The situation would still be the same, and all Simon was doing was postponing the inevitable. He was just being infuriatingly stubborn and implacable. Because nothing, not even if Kinray turned out to be another Garden of Eden, was going to persuade her to leave London!

CHAPTER THREE

THEY left London for Scotland the following Friday evening, and even Cassie had to admit that the journey was fairly painless. A company chauffeur called to pick them up and drive them to Heathrow Airport where a twelve-seater plane, again owned by Mullaine's, was waiting to take them and ten others to Glasgow. There was no baggage check-in to queue at, no sitting around in the departure lounge for the usual interminable wait, they were just ushered into a private room and given a drink while their luggage was put on board, then taken out to the plane with the others and took off within minutes. The plane was smooth and luxurious, even if it seemed incredibly small after all the large airliners that Cassie was used to on holiday trips, and there was an attractive young stewardess to see to their needs.

Cassie looked the stewardess over, noting her pretty face, slim figure and trim ankles, and decided that she was too pretty. The other men on the flight—she was the only woman passenger—all seemed to find the girl attractive too, one or two of them openly trying to chat her up, and Cassie wondered wryly just what they got up to while they were away from home. Simon had told her that most of the workers had a contract in which they worked every day for three weeks, then had a whole week off. From the look of some of the men they were no saints, and she could imagine them getting up to all sorts of mischief when they were away from home for so long.

The stewardess brought them drinks and Cassie watched Simon as he took his, murmuring a word of thanks. For the first time in their marriage it occurred to Cassie to wonder if he, too, was ever unfaithful to her during his frequent trips away from home. Certainly the opportunity was there, for it was obvious from the way the girl had looked him over when they boarded the plane that she found him attractive, and would much prefer a young, handsome junior executive to any of the rather crude labourers who were trying to chat her up. But beyond giving her a brief smile of thanks, Simon showed no interest in her at all, merely turning his eyes immediately back to the report he was reading.

Cassie accepted her own drink and sat back in her seat, laughing at herself for being a fool. Simon had no need to even look at another woman, had he? Not when their sex life was so good, so completely satisfying. In fact they had had very few differences, really, in all the three years of their marriage. Small things, of course, at the beginning, when they'd been getting used to living together, to being a couple instead of individuals. But nothing major. Nothing till now, that was.

She sighed and Simon turned to look at her. 'Tired?'

'No, not really. Will we be staying at the house you told me about, the site director's house?'

'No, at a hotel. The house won't be available until the other man moves out at the end of the mouth. But I've arranged for you to look it over.'

For a second Cassie was tempted to say again that it was all a waste of time, but reiterating the obvious wasn't going to help; it would only put Simon's back up and make the weekend even more unpleasant than it was already. She tried to think of something else to talk about, but couldn't, so took a long sip of her drink. After a moment Simon turned away and resumed his reading.

They spent that night at a hotel in Glasgow, leaving there immediately after breakfast the next morning to be taken by helicopter to the site at Kinray. It was the first time Cassie had ever flown in a helicopter and she felt more than a little nervous. It seemed so much more unwieldy than a plane, and the engine was so noisy that she wanted to put her hands over her ears, but they were already occupied in tightly gripping the arms of her seat.

'The helicopter is a godsend to the oil industry,' Simon remarked as the machine started to rise. 'They're used continuously, especially ferrying men and equipment to the oil rigs out in the sea. Rather like a bus service, really, only far more reliable and efficient than London Transport, of course.'

His hand came down to cover hers, warm and comforting, while he went on talking, gently reassuring her by his choice of words, letting her know that he knew she was afraid, but that the flight was a safe, everyday occurrence.

'Look out of the window,' he went on. 'When you're only this high everything looks as if it's on a model scale, as if you're a giant with the whole earth to play with.'

Reluctantly Cassie turned her head to look out of the window and, after the first hesitant glance, immediately became fascinated as she saw the airport reduced to toy size below them. But everything was in such perfect detail: the planes waiting to take off, little vans being driven up to unload them, tiny men in white overalls hurrying along like ants on an anthill. This was, she supposed, what the term 'bird's eye view' was all about.

They were in the air for almost half an hour, flying to the north-west across Scotland's rivered valleys and deep green, rolling hills, most of them still capped by snow, until they were suddenly at the coast with the surging grey sea below them.

'There's the site.'

Simon pointed over to the right and for a moment Cassie thought it was a large seaside town they were approaching, but then she saw the massive round oil storage tanks, some already built, others in the process of construction and the other mass of building work, the whole covering a huge area of land.

'Fly us round the site before you land, will you?' Simon instructed the pilot, who nodded and banked the helicopter into a steep turn that took them round the perimeter of the massive site. 'Down there, out to sea, you can see where the jetties for loading and unloading oil tankers are being built,' Simon told her. 'There will be three initially, with a fourth being built later. We expect to have up to twenty crude oil-carrying tankers a week when the terminal is fully operational, and also a smaller number of gas carriers.' He pointed again as the helicopter turned away from the sea. 'That building there is the terminal's own power station which is essential to give us the power to run the separation plant.' He saw her blank look and added, 'Coming ashore in the crude oil will be a mixture of hydrocarbon liquids, dissolved gases, and some water, so we have to separate the gas and water from the oil to yield products that can safely be transported.'

He went on to point out other aspects of the site,

but Cassie listened with only half an ear. Her mind was taking in this new aspect of her husband; a man who was an expert in his job and who had been offered the control of this whole huge operation that lay spread below her like some huge-scale map. She also noticed how he used the possessive pronoun when talking about it, and realised that he was already deeply involved in the project, even if not yet part of it.

The helicopter finished its circle of the site and flew on for about a mile towards a group of buildings that this time *did* turn out to be a small town with its own airport.

'This is Kinray village,' Simon told her. 'The construction company we took over from built it to house all the workers on the site before they started the terminal. They finished it some time ago and it's already settled down into being a community—as much as a place can be, that is, when most of its inhabitants are constantly changing.'

The helicopter settled down gently on the landing pad, the rotor blades coming to a halt as the engine was switched off. Cassie found the ensuing silence an almost physical release. Some steps were wheeled up to the door and Simon took her hand as she climbed rather stiffly down.

'Good morning, Mrs Ventris—or may I call you Cassie? Remember me, I'm Patrick Bright, the Financial Director of Mullaine's.'

'Yes, of course. How are you, Mr Bright?'

'Oh, please, call me Patrick.'

He took her arm, a short amiable-looking man of about forty-five whose keen financial brain was belied by his appearance. Cassie had met him only a few times before at various official functions and was rather overwhelmed that this member of Mullaine's hierarchy was making such a fuss of her. He led her to a car, sat down beside her and insisted on spreading a rug over her knees.

'It's just a short drive to the hotel, won't take more than a few minutes,' he told her as Simon got in at her other side.

It was, as he'd said, a short drive, and he kept talking the whole time so that Cassie had to give him her attention and she had little opportunity to notice her surroundings, but she did catch fleeting glimpses of the 'village', and she got the impression of raw newness, of grey prefabricated buildings thrown up in haste, with no sort of architectural embellishments, just large barrack-like blocks adapted for different uses; a parade of shops, a post office, a garage, and several that were obviously hostels for the single men who numbered the greater part of the large work force.

The hotel was a little better; some thought had been given to its design and it resembled some of the more modern London hotels, all tinted glass and variegated concrete, which was supposed to give it individuality.

A rush of cold air whipped round her as she got out of the car, but there was hardly time for it to penetrate her fur jacket before Patrick Bright had hurried her into the centrally-heated warmth of the hotel. This, at first, was comfortingly warm, but then began to feel rather oppressive so that she soon slipped off her jacket as the hotel manager himself came forward to greet them and then led them into a lounge where Patrick Bright ordered coffee.

'Thought you might like a hot drink before you go up to your room. Don't worry about your suitcase, the porter will have taken it up.'

The coffee came almost at once, as if the order had been anticipated, the waiter and the hotel manager fussing around them to make sure they had everything they wanted.

'Of course, you've got to remember,' Patrick was saying, 'that Kinray is very much a new town. And unfortunately most of the accommodation buildings had already been put up when we took over, so we had no say in their design, and,' he leant forward confidentially, 'quite frankly, Cassie, they're extremely ugly. But now that we've taken over we hope to improve matters and we've already started building a new sports complex to take the place of the inadequate facilities they had before. The new complex is going to have indoor tennis and squash courts, an ice hockey stadium, a bowling alley, as well as an Olympic-sized swimming pool. You name it, we've got it,' he added, with some pride.

'It all sounds wonderful,' Cassie said politely, because he obviously expected her to make some such comment. 'For people who are interested in sport, that is.'

'Oh, we haven't forgotten the arts and sciences either,' the older man told her. 'We have two large cinemas, a theatre where good touring companies can put on their shows, musical as well as theatrical. Then, of course, there's an extremely good library, one of the best for a place this size that there is in Scotland.'

'Well, I expect there's plenty of time to read; the nights in winter are extremely long, aren't they?'

She spoke civilly enough, but there was an edge to her voice that Simon picked up at once. He had been sitting silently, letting Patrick Bright take over the conversation, but now he glanced quickly at her and realised from the set look on her face that she was becoming annoyed by the hard sell she was being given. He went to say something, but before he could do so Patrick Bright said over-heartily, 'But we have an extremely active social life here—lots of parties, a bridge club and a drama group, that kind of thing. More organisations than you have the time to go to. My wife always has a very enjoyable time whenever she comes up here.'

'Yes, but then she doesn't have to live here, does she?'

He got it then, realised that he was overdoing it, and immediately stood up, glancing at his watch. 'Well, if you'll excuse me, I have an appointment shortly. And I expect you'd like to get settled into your room. But I hope you'll join me here in the restaurant for lunch at one, and then we've arranged for you to have a tour round Kinray.'

He took his leave and Cassie and Simon immediately went up to their room. Cassie was silent as they went up in the lift with the porter who was showing them the way, waiting until he'd shown them into the room. Only it wasn't just a room, it was a suite, with a large sitting-room as well as a luxurious bathroom and a beautifully furnished bedroom with twin beds under gold-coloured counterpanes. On a side table there was a complimentary bottle of champagne in an ice bucket, together with a large box of chocolates, a packet of Scottish shortbread and a basket of fruit. There were flowers, too, in both the sitting-room and the bedroom. Ordinarily to stay in such luxury would have thrilled and excited Cassie, but right then it only added to her anger, to the feeling that she was being wooed into accepting something she didn't want. So as soon as the porter had gone she turned on Simon angrily.

'If you think I'm going to . . '

But he stopped her by the simple expedient of coming up to her and kissing her hard on the mouth. For a moment she tried to resist him, but he put a hand on the back of her head, pressing her against him, and after a few minutes she reluctantly opened her mouth and was instantly lost to everything else.

When eventually he let her go she stood still in his arms, her body quivering. Slowly she lifted her head to look at him.

'That wasn't fair!'

He grinned. 'No, it wasn't, was it? But at least it gave me the chance to get a word in before you erupted.'

Cassie stiffened. 'I had a perfect right to be angry.'

'I know. I quite agree.'

'You do?' She looked at him in some astonishment.

'Yes. Poor old Patrick overdid it, I'm afraid. But you'll have to forgive him; he really is enthusiastic about this project and wants it to be carried out as quickly and efficiently as possible. And if having me in charge of construction is going to help, then he'll do everything in his power to help bring that about.'

'Including giving your less than enthusiastic wife the hard sell,' Cassie said accusingly.

Simon shrugged. 'To him it isn't a hard sell. He genuinely believes that we're creating something worthwhile here, a place that provides every need of the workers and more—a place where even a London businesswoman would find enough entertainment and not be bored.'

Cassie stepped back out of his arms and glared up at him. 'If that's supposed to mean that I'm too snobbish or stubborn to accept what there is here, then you're wrong. I'm quite capable of filling my time and entertaining myself, if necessary.'

His eyebrows rising quizzically, Simon said, 'But even so, you're still quite convinced that you'd be bored here, aren't you?'

'Yes.' Cassie turned away and took a few paces round the room, then turned to him, her hands opening towards him in a pleading gesture as she tried to make him understand. 'Because what's offered here is only entertainment, a means of passing the time. Oh, perhaps pleasantly enough, if you really let yourself get involved. But that's all it is. There's no creative stimulus, no challenge. Nothing to make you go to bed feeling satisfied and fulfilled by the work you've done during the day. Nothing to make you look forward to tomorrow. Even if I filled every minute of my days here, I'd still only feel that I was marking time, just filling in the hours of waiting until I could get back to London and start living again.'

She came to an abrupt stop, her face flushed, her green eyes gazing earnestly up into his. After a moment, she added, 'You do understand, don't you?'

Simon laughed mirthlessly. 'Oh, yes, I understand all right. Though it's not easy for a man to accept that he takes second place to his wife's work!'

Cassie stared up at him in consternation. 'But that isn't what I meant at all. That doesn't come into it.'

'Doesn't it? I seem to remember you saying, before we were married, that you loved me so much that you'd follow me anywhere I went. But it seems that that only applies so long as it's in the environs of London,' he added with bitter irony.

Green eyes flashing, Cassie said heatedly, 'Oh, for

heaven's sake stop it! You're taking this personally, when there's nothing personal about it. If you'd been offered a post in some other city where I could have got a similar job I would have gone with you willingly. And if you want to quote what we said in the past, wasn't it you who said that all you wanted in the world was to make me happy? Well, I wouldn't be happy here.' She shook her head helplessly. 'I've tried to explain to you how I feel. I'm sorry if you don't like it, but that's the way it is.'

She gazed at Simon, half unhappy, half defiant, waiting for him to speak. For a long moment he stood, hands shoved in his pockets, looking at her broodingly, then he sighed, came over to her and pulled her to him, her head on his shoulder. Ruefully he said, 'You're right, neither of us can help it. We're both products of our age. You fighting for equality, and me agreeing in principle that you should have it, but the first time our paths diverge expecting you to conform to the traditional feminine image and give up everything for me.' He gave a wry grin. 'Selfish, aren't I?'

Cassie smiled back up at him, relief in her face. 'A typical male chauvinist pig.'

He laughed and kissed her nose. 'We'd better unpack or we'll be late for lunch.'

'Do you still want me to go on the tour this afternoon?'

'I think you owe that much to Mullaine's—if not to me.'

Simon spoke lightly, but those last four words made Cassie realise that no matter how much he pretended otherwise, he still saw her defiance on a personal level, still brought the issue down to the basis of she either loved him enough to give everything up for him or she didn't. Really, to Simon, it was as simple as that.

Opening the suitcase, Cassie took out her make-up bag and went into the bathroom, locking the door behind her. She turned on the tap but didn't immediately begin to wash, just stood and stared at herself in the mirror. Why did life have to be so complicated? You were going along happily with everything fine and even getting better, and then, suddenly— wham!—life hit you in the face and knocked you down again. And it was all because of Simon's stubbornness. He must have known, even before he'd asked her, that she would never consent. Slipping off her sweater, she began to wash and then re-do her make-up, taking her time about it, for the first time since she'd known him feeling so angry with her husband that she wished he'd just go away and leave her alone.

Lunch wasn't an easy meal, nor the tour after it, but Patrick Bright had obviously realised his mistake and managed to keep down his salesman's patter, while Simon—bearing in mind the temper that went with her tawny hair and green eyes—had advised her to play it cool. 'After all, Patrick is my boss,' he reminded her. So somehow they got through the afternoon with Cassie obediently inspecting every amenity including even the half-finished sports complex and making suitable remarks whenever she could think of them. Actually, if anything, she was rather impressed with all the facilities available for the construction workers, and to a lesser extent, for the small percentage of people who lived permanently in Kinray. Permanently in most cases, of course, being for the two to three years it would take to build the terminal. Then the number of workers would gradually decrease until their places were taken by the maintenance and specialist people who would man and operate the oil terminal and its jetties when these were fully functional. Just a very small number in comparison to the thousands who were here now. Yes, the facilities were ideal for men who had done a hard day's physical work and just wanted to sit back and be amused, but there was nothing here that could attract Cassie, nothing that wouldn't make each day spent here a small, individual hell of boredom and frustration.

Dinner that night was easier, because three other couples had been invited together with Patrick Bright's secretary to keep the numbers even. They ate in a private room in the hotel, the food was good, there was plenty of wine and the atmosphere soon became relaxed and congenial, so that it was gone midnight before they went up to their room. Cassie flopped down in an armchair and kicked off her shoes, more than a little inebriated. Rifling through the box of chocolates, she found one with a nut centre and put it in her mouth.

'Mm, I could get used to this kind of treatment,' she told Simon mumblingly.

'Didn't your mother ever teach you not to speak with your mouth full?' he demanded with a mock frown.

Cassie wrinkled her nose at him, but swallowed the sweet. 'Do you stay at this hotel every time you come up here?'

'Yes, in this suite sometimes. Shall we open the champagne?'

'We might as well. Another couple of drinks aren't going to make any difference after what we've had already.' She waited until Simon had opened the bottle, the cork flying off with a satisfying bang. 'It must seem rather a come-down to go home after this,' she remarked, not looking at him.

Simon glanced at her sharply, then answered, 'The service here is certainly very good and the food is always excellent.' He paused, and Cassie thought of all the meals she'd ruined or dished up out of tins at the last minute. 'But,' Simon went on smoothly, 'I must say that the chambermaid service one gets at home is much, much better.' And he came to put a hand on each arm of her chair and lean over to kiss her.

Cassie laughed and put her arms round his neck. 'Oh, the hotel doesn't provide *everything*, then?'

'Not as far as I'm concerned.' He straightened up and gave her her glass of champagne.

She watched him as he took off his jacket and tie, as always at this point beginning to be sexually aware, knowing every inch of the powerful body concealed by his clothes. She sipped her champagne, watching him, but then an intriguing thought occurred to her. 'Simon? You said that Mullaine's doesn't provide everything as far as *you're* concerned. But does it for everyone else? I mean—all those single men who work here? Is there a—you know—a place for them to go to?'

Simon had his back to her and she didn't see the flash of laughter that came into his eyes, but, schooling his features, he turned a bland face towards her and was deliberately vague. 'A place?'

'Yes. You know—a place where they can meet girls.'

'Well, there's a dance every Saturday night. I believe quite a few local girls go there.'

'No,' Cassie shook her head impatiently, 'I meant a place where they can go to—well, have sex. A—a brothel.' She flushed as she said it and looked up to find Simon grinning widely. Setting down her glass, she jumped up and ran to hit him on the chest with her fists. 'You beast, you knew what I meant all the time!'

'Yes, but it was more fun trying to get you to say it.' He put his arms round her and kissed her. 'My darling girl, if you want to ask a question like that then you've got to come right out and say it. It only becomes embarrassing when you beat around the bush like that.'

'Well, you still haven't answered me. Do they have a brothel here?'

Simon laughed and picked her up. 'Of course they don't. This site is in the centre of a moral God-fearing community. They'd have the whole project closed down at the merest hint of such a thing. No, the men go home to their wives and girl-friends to satisfy their sexual appetites. Just as I,' he added, making for the bedroom, 'am going to satisfy mine.'

'And mine, I hope,' Cassie put in, her arms round his neck, her mouth biting his ear.

'Oh, most definitely yours as well.' He stopped to kiss her, then picked up the bottle of champagne. 'Let's finish the rest of this in bed, shall we? Why don't you put out the light?'

Cassie obeyed and he carried her into the bedroom, shouldering the door shut behind them. Setting her down, he began to undress her, his fingers sure and skilled. Cassie let him for a while and then she, too, began to undress him, but her hands often stopping to touch, explore, until Simon grabbed her hands and exclaimed, 'You little hussy! Get in bed before I take you here and now.'

She pulled a petulant face, put her arms round his neck and moved her breasts against his bare chest so that his hairs softly tickled her. 'I don't like single beds,' she complained.

'Oh, but in single beds you have to stay very, very close all night,' Simon told her as he pulled back the covers and helped her in.

'All night? You promise?'

He laughed. 'That's not just a promise, sweetheart, that's a certainty. Move over and I'll show you.'

And he did, most satisfactorily.

But it was cramped in the small bed and when Cassie awoke early in the morning and tried to turn, she woke Simon as well. He grunted and reached out for her.

'No,' Cassie mumbled, still more than half asleep. 'It's too early.'

He chuckled and kissed her ear. 'Always knew you wouldn't be able to stand the pace!'

'You're lying on my arm, it hurts.'

'Okay, okay, I can take a hint.' He got out of bed and climbed into the other one. 'God, this feels cold. The things I do for you!'

'Oh, shut up and go to sleep.' Cassie yawned and spread herself luxuriously, then almost immediately fell asleep again as Simon laughed at her bullying tone.

It was just as well they had split up, because a few hours later a maid brought them up breakfast and the papers, courtesy of Mullaine's, of course. Cassie was no prude, but she didn't relish being gossiped about by workers at the hotel. Not that they were directly employed by Mullaine's, because another group had the hotel concession, but she could well imagine that in a close-knit community such as this, everyone already knew that Simon had been offered the post of site director, and that she had come up to Kinray to look the place over.

'Good heavens!' she exclaimed. 'They've sent us up *all* the Sunday papers. We'll be able to have a colour supplement each, instead of fighting over it.'

Cassie took her time over breakfast and getting dressed, and Simon didn't hurry her, although he was ready long before she was, sitting stretched out in the armchair reading one of the papers more thoroughly. It was perverse of her to take so long, because she knew that they were due to look over the site director's house at eleven and it was almost that already. But some instinct told her that even now Simon was clinging to a last-ditch hope that she would see the house and be willing to live there. He wasn't the type to give up easily, of course, she'd always known that, and for him to have to accept defeat would be very hard, especially as he wanted this job, wanted it badly. This weekend, if it had done nothing else, had shown her that. And because she loved him and didn't want to hurt him, she was reluctant for the time to come when she would have to say that last, definite no.

At last she couldn't procrastinate any longer and turned to him. 'I'm ready.'

He folded the paper neatly and stood up, looking her over sardonically. 'You're quite sure you haven't forgotten anything?'

Cassie flushed, knowing the barb was deserved, but said steadily, 'No, I don't think so.'

'Let's go, then.'

He took her arm and led her down to the foyer where the chauffeur was waiting. He had been waiting some time and apologised because the car had got cold, which made Cassie feel rotten. They drove out of Kinray and skirted the long perimeter of the construction site, the house being to the south of the oil terminal. The morning was cold and frosty but very clear, and as they drove the sun came out, turning the frozen puddles at the side of the road into eye-dazzling mirrors. Once past the construction site, they turned off the new wide highway that had been specially built to supply it, on to a much narrower road only wide enough for cars to pass at special places every quarter of a mile or so where the road had been widened. The road wound through a kind of pass between the hills, hills that were dark grey and inhospitable, the white of snow nestling in the deeper fissures of rock where the sun didn't penetrate. There was very little flora on the hills, just the dry brown sticks of heather plants, their flowers long faded.

As they rounded the shoulder of a hill, the car descended into a valley, and to her surprise Cassie saw that there were trees there, mostly firs and evergreens, growing in an area sheltered from the wind. The road ran through them and then turned in between stone pillars leading up to a house. The road didn't go past the entrance, it led only to the house. They came out of the trees and Cassie saw the sea on her right, with a long open sweep of land leading down to it, bordered on both sides by the gentle slopes of the hills. She was sitting on the right-hand side of the car so had a perfect view as they drove along, and she didn't even turn to see the house until the car drew up outside and the chauffeur got out to open the door for them.

The house was the type that you either fell in love with immediately or couldn't stand at any price. It was built of the same grey stone as the hills, mellowed by time and its harshness softened by the rich greenness of ivy, and had a front door set into a sort of rounded turret to one side. It was old, probably eighteenth or early nineteenth century, and three-storied, with the top storey windows set into small gables in the roof. The original windows in the rest of the house were also small, probably to let in less of the sea winds, but some on the ground floor had been enlarged at some time and there were also patio doors set into a corresponding turret at the other side of the house, leading into a garden. Not so much a garden in the English sense with neat flower beds, lawns and shrubberies, but a long expanse of rough grass hedged on each side by wilderness-like areas of spindly trees and rhododendron bushes, but with the view to the sea left open and uninterrupted so that the smell of it came clear to Cassie's nostrils on the light breeze.

A woman had come to the door at the sound of the car and for a moment Cassie thought she was going to have the embarrassing experience of meeting the woman whose husband Simon had been asked to replace. But it was soon made clear that the woman was only the maid.

'Mr and Mrs Richards are at the kirk,' she informed them in a broad Highland accent. 'They told me to show you over the house.'

The house was large, much bigger than Cassie had expected, and was well looked after and modernised.

'This was originally the local laird's house,' Simon told her. 'He owned nearly the whole of Kinray and all the land that the terminal's being built on. When our predecessors bought it he moved out and went to live in the Bahamas on the proceeds, and the company fully renovated and modernised this house. I understand that it had been rather neglected for some time before that.'

'Och, that it was, sir,' the maid, Mrs Campbell, confirmed. 'The old laird didn't have a spare penny to spend on it, and now they say he's a millionaire.'

Cassie looked at the middle-aged woman curiously. 'Didn't you mind the oil terminal being built here?'

'No, indeed,' the maid replied warmly. 'I've a husband and three grown sons, and all of them out of work for years until the oil came.'

She took them up the wide wooden staircase and insisted on showing them every corner of the house, right up into the top storey bedrooms and down to the cellar before Simon thanked and gently dismissed her and she reluctantly left them alone. They were standing in what was probably the best room in the house. It had a high, ornately plastered ceiling and the partly-panelled walls were hung with a series of flower paintings. The floor was of polished oak partly covered by a beautiful Indian carpet and the room was warmed by the rich dark red velvet of the curtains as well as by the bright log fire which burnt in the hearth and the sun which shone through the sparklingly clean window panes. The furniture was mostly antique, but the settee and armchairs were comfortable-looking modern reproductions in a pastel pink flowered pattern.

But however beautiful the room, it was the view that drew Cassie's gaze. She walked over to the deep window embrasure with its red-cushioned seat and looked down the long vista of the garden to where the greenness of grass gave way to the soft amber of sand and the scintillating lines of light that marked the crest of each wave as it moved into the shore, only to burst into myriad rainbows of spray as they broke on the beach.

For a while they both stood silently, then Cassie sighed and said, 'You were right, it is beautiful.'

Simon came up behind her and put his hands on her shoulders. 'I'm glad you like it.'

He spoke lightly, but Cassie could feel the tension in his fingers as he waited for her to give her decision. And it would have been so easy to have given in, to say, Yes, all right, I'll do what you want. I'll give up my job and come here with you. And for a while it would have been worth it, to see Simon's face light up with happiness and triumph and have him show her how much he loved her for it. But she knew that it wouldn't be long before this beautiful house would seem like a prison and her naturally happy disposition begin to be eaten away by frustration and bitterness. She loved Simon very much, but she didn't know if it was strong enough to survive something like that. She owed it to them both to be honest, to say how she really felt.

Simon was saying. 'I've never seen such a magnificent piece of landscape.'

Deliberately Cassie moved out of his hold and turned to face him. 'No. But who was it who said that landscape can become extremely tedious when that's all there is?'

He looked at her for a moment, then shoved his hands in his trouser pockets; a habit he had when he didn't want to show his emotions. 'Does that mean what I suppose it does?'

'That I won't come to live here? Yes, I'm afraid it does.'

He gave a short, mirthless laugh. 'I was stupid to hope that this place would change your mind, I suppose, but nevertheless I clung to that. I thought that if anything could persuade you it would be this house.'

'I'm sorry,' Cassie said inadequately. 'I know how

much you want this job and will hate having to give it up, but I just can't live here, Simon.'

Pulling a packet of cigarettes from his pocket, he lit one and drew hard on it. He was still standing by the window, looking out, but his expression was abstracted, as if his thoughts were miles away. When at length he did turn to her there was a cold, withdrawn look on his face.

'All right, then I'll just have to accept the fact. But I'm afraid I'm not going to turn this job down, Cassie. Not just because it's too good an opportunity to miss, but because I've already got so involved with this project that I've got to see it through. I can't give it up any more than you can give up your job.'

'B-but you can't!' Cassie exclaimed, her brow wrinkling in perplexity. 'I've said no. I . . .'

'I know what you said,' Simon cut in, 'but it doesn't make any difference. Tomorrow I'm going to tell the board of directors that I'll accept the job.'

Cassie stared at him, her face hostile. 'Is this some kind of ultimatum? Are you *ordering* me to come and live here?'

Simon's mouth twisted wryly and he sounded suddenly tired. 'No, I'm not issuing any commands. Unfortunately you're one of the few people here that I can't order around. Ironic, isn't it?' he added bitterly. He drew on his cigarette, then looked at it and ground it out in an ashtray as if he suddenly found it distasteful. 'No, I'm simply saying that you've made your decision and I've made mine. We both want different things and neither of us is willing to make any concessions. So we'll just have to go our separate ways instead of being together.'

His words made Cassie feel suddenly very, very cold.

Her face paled and her voice stuck in her throat as she said, 'What do you mean?'

Simon turned to face her. 'That I'll live and work here while you go on living in the flat in London. I'll fly down as often as I can at the weekends, of course, but I may not be able to get away every weekend, especially at the beginning, but perhaps you could come up here sometimes. If that wouldn't be asking too much, of course,' he added cynically.

Cassie's first reaction was the overwhelming rush of relief one always feels when a great fear is suddenly removed. Her heart began to beat again and colour rushed into her cheeks.

'Oh, Simon!' She ran to him and threw her arms round his neck, pressed closely against him. 'I'm sorry, I'm so sorry.'

His arms came round her and held her tightly, but he didn't speak.

Lifting her head, her eyes close to tears, Cassie said haltingly, 'Isn't there any alternative? I don't want us to be apart.'

Ruefully, Simon shook his head. 'Nor do I, darling. But I can't see any other way for us both to get what we want out of life.'

'But for three years! It will seem like a lifetime.' She put her hands on his shoulders and looked up at him worriedly. 'And what guarantee would we have that Mullaine's wouldn't send you off somewhere else when this project is finished?'

'A lot can happen in three years,' Simon reminded her. 'And by then, if I've made a success of this, I'll have a bit more weight to throw about with the other directors.' He put his hand up and wiped a tear from her cheek. 'Don't worry; we'll both be busy, the time will soon pass, and we'll see each other as often as we can. Then I'll make sure we're together.'

'Promise?'

'Promise.' He bent and put his mouth on hers, sealing the promise with a kiss.

Slowly Cassie opened her eyes to look at him, studying each feature of his face all over again, realising that from that moment on their lives, their whole relationship, was going to change. Up until now she had been so happy, had had everything she'd ever wanted. Even now she had, she supposed, again got what she wanted, and couldn't help feeling a surge of satisfaction because of it, but she had had no idea that Simon would ever decide on such a solution. That he could even contemplate it startled and at first appalled her. Never in her wildest imaginings had she dreamt that they would live apart, but as she thought about it she realised that it made sense, and Simon was right, the time would soon pass, and they would see each other as much as possible, almost as much as they did now really, because Simon was so often away. As they left the house and walked to the waiting car, Cassie felt almost cheerful again. Even if they were apart, at least there was no conflict between them any more, there were holidays and lots of other times together to look forward to—and, she thought with satisfaction, she could now give her whole attention to the improvements she wanted to make in the fashion departments at Marriott & Brown's.

CHAPTER FOUR

AT first Cassie hardly missed Simon; it was just like all the other times when he was away somewhere sorting out problems for Mullaine's, and she didn't feel at all lonely. They spoke on the telephone nearly every night, but this gradually became every other and then once every three or four nights as they ran out of new things to talk about. They each listened politely when the other talked about work and its difficulties, but perhaps they both sensed that the interest was only cursory, that their minds were too full of their own problems to pay any real attention to the other's.

He was unable to get away for the first three weekends and Cassie voluntarily spent the Saturdays in the store, going through the stock lists in the departments she'd taken over and deciding on what lines she wanted to replace them. Unfortunately, from her point of view, the January sales were over and Mrs Nichols had already stocked up with new merchandise, so it would take a month or two before she could put her own plans into operation, but at least it gave her plenty of time to decide on exactly what she wanted. In the evenings she worked late, often not getting home until eight or nine o'clock, when she either opened a couple of tins or else took a ready-meal from the freezer and just heated it up, and sat and ate it in front of the television, too tired to do anything else but let the screen's flickerings lull her into a soporific, semi-trancelike state until she rolled into bed.

This was fine for a while, but gradually the pressure of work eased as she took full control of the new departments and became familiar with their staff and needs. She decided to concentrate on modernising one department at a time, and decided to start with the swimwear department as that was the smallest and was just coming into its own again after the winter rundown. She had a talk with the girls working there, finding them keen and enthusiastic about her new ideas and making sure that they were behind her. It was a policy she had always adopted and found that it generally worked well, especially among the younger members of staff, although there were always a few diehards among the people who had worked there for years and didn't see any point in changing tried and tested lines and methods. 'But we've always displayed that model there,' one would complain when Cassie told her to move the headless and limbless torso clad in a pink, boned corselet.

'Yes, but now I want to put one of the more lifelike models with the latest silk French knickers and lace bras there. You see, it's near the escalator and we want the model to catch the eye of women going up to the next floor and draw them into this department,' Cassie would explain patiently, adding a clinching, 'After all, the more people we get in here the more are likely to buy something, and then your commission goes up, doesn't it?'

It was stimulating and exciting and Cassie loved it, but gradually she began to feel a little restless and lonely, began to wish that Simon would come home. Of course there was always Sue Martin, her assistant, with whom she could have lunch or slip into a pub with for a drink before going home, and a couple of times she went on shopping trips with Julia Russell, or some other friend, but it was in the evenings, especially when she lay alone in bed, that she really felt lonely. She would lie in the big double bed, tossing and turning restlessly, unable to get to sleep even though she was both mentally and physically tired, and it gradually dawned on her that it wasn't only Simon she missed so much but also his lovemaking. Both of them had a high sex drive and made love often when he was home, Simon—by far the more experienced—always able to bring her to a dizzying climax time after time. And she missed that, missed the joyous ecstasy of sex and missed just being near to him, held close in his arms, feeling his strong male body against hers and anticipating with certain excitement the rapture to come.

But when he did come home it was only for a fleeting visit and most of the precious few hours were spent at the office. Also it was the wrong time of the month, so Cassie felt, if anything, even more frustrated when she went with him in the car to see him off at the airport.

'Surely they can spare you for at least another day,' she complained as they drew up outside the air terminal. 'It's ridiculous coming all this way just for twenty-four hours.'

Simon put his arm round her and drew her to him, put his face against her hair, savouring its clean, sweet smell. 'It's all I could manage, love. Do you think I wouldn't have stayed longer if I could possibly have arranged it?'

'When will you be able to get home again?'

He shrugged. 'I just can't say, I'm afraid. At the moment we're working out a whole new pay structure

system with the unions that we hope will settle all our
labour difficulties once and for all. But as there are
over a dozen different unions involved in various jobs
on the site it's no easy matter to get them all in agree-
ment. Often you think you're really getting somewhere
when one union will bring up a point that throws them
all into disruption again.' He grinned wryly and went
to go on, but glanced at Cassie's face and then sat back,
withdrawing his arm. 'But you don't want to know
about that.'

For a second she almost made the mistake of agreeing with him, but just in time saw the tight look in
his face and was filled with a sudden surge of love and
need. Impulsively she leaned over and grabbed the
lapels of his overcoat, saying fiercely, 'I do, if it's
what's keeping us apart. You've never been away for
so long before and I miss you.' She kissed him, her
lips urgent. 'And I want you. Oh, Simon, I want you
so much!'

His arms went round her again as he returned her
kiss, answering her urgency with a fierce need of his
own, his arms hurting her as he crushed her to him.
After he at length raised his head, he still held her
close, her head against his shoulder as he put up a
hand to gently stroke her face, to smooth back a lock
of hair. His voice thick, he said, 'Look, try and get up
to Scotland next weekend, okay? I'll try and arrange
for the firm to fly you up.'

'Oh, but next Saturday I was going to have a meeting
with the window dressers to decide on how to display
the new Spring collection.' She felt his fingers tighten
against her face and saw a bleak, closed-in look come
into his eyes. Impulsively she reached up and caught
his wrist just as he was about to withdraw his hand.

'All right, I'll come. It will be the devil's own job to get everyone to stay behind one evening after work instead, but I'll manage it somehow.'

Immediately his eyes grew warm and he kissed her again. 'That's great. I'll lay it on with the firm.'

He went to get out of the car, but Cassie stopped him. 'Wait. What clothes will I need? Is it still cold up there? What will we be doing?'

Simon grinned, a devilish light in his eyes. 'Just bring your sexiest nightdress. Because I'm going to take you to bed and we're going to stay there for the whole weekend!'

Cassie laughed and pretended to be a little shocked, but as she drove back to the West End she felt gay and bubbly with inner excitement, glad that she'd promised to go even though it meant asking several people to reorganise their schedules just to achieve it. As soon as she reached the store she asked Sue Martin to get the first of the people on the phone.

'Shall I talk to them?' Sue offered.

'No, I'd better speak to them myself; they'll be upset enough at having to change the time of the meeting, better not make it worse by delegating the job to you.' As Sue dialled the number, Cassie added, 'How about you, Sue? I know you were going to come to the Saturday meeting, but I expect you'll want to get home to Chris in the evening, won't you?'

Her assistant pulled a wry face. 'Oh, there's no hurry. Chris seems to be working late at the office quite a bit lately, much more than he used to.'

'Is there a special job on or something?'

'Not really. He said that someone left rather suddenly and hasn't yet been replaced, so he's having to take on an extra work-load. He even had to go into the office last Saturday and again this week.'

'Well, I'm sure his firm will appreciate him helping
them out, and it all helps in the promotion stakes. Look
on it as logging up some credit for the future,' Cassie
said encouragingly, adding, 'Anyway, I don't expect it
will be for long.'

'I hope not,' Sue answered glumly. 'I'm getting fed
up with being by myself. What's the point of being
married if you can't be together?'

Cassie looked at the younger girl sharply, but she
was too wrapped up in her own problems to realise
that her remark also applied to Cassie's situation. Then
the person Cassie wanted to speak to came on the line,
so the two girls were plunged back into the work rou-
tine, their domestic difficulties for the moment
shelved.

The rest of that week was both hectic and frustrating, with things seeming to go wrong all the time
and one problem being solved only to have several
more crop up. And this happened at home as well as in
the office: first the television went into fuzzy lines and
then Cassie got a panic phone call from the people in
the flat below and she rushed home to find that the
washing machine, which she'd left working happily,
had gone wrong and was continually pouring out water
that had flooded the kitchen and spread to the sitting-
room carpet. Cassie managed to turn the water off and
mop up the worst of the mess, but then had to dash
back to the store to interview a salesman who had come
all the way from Denmark and had only stopped over
on his way to America.

By the time Friday evening came all she wanted to
do was put her feet up, but she had arranged with
Mullaine's for a car to pick her up straight from work,

but of course there was—inevitably for that ghastly week—a last-minute phone call with another problem she had to solve, so the car was left waiting for half an hour and then there was a mad panic to get through the Friday night rush hour traffic of workers trying to get home while others were driving into the West End to do some window-shopping or to have a meal before going on to a show or cinema. The driver was none too pleased with her and let his annoyance show by making the ride as rough and jerky as possible, taking corners too fast so that she had to hold on to the strap to stop herself swinging across the car and putting on his brakes sharply at traffic lights so that she shot forward in her seat.

When she got to Heathrow she was seething with anger and would have given the driver a piece of her mind if he hadn't thwarted her by dumping her case on the pavement and immediately getting back in and driving off, leaving her staring after him, fuming with annoyance. Cassie picked up her case and walked towards the area for private flights, trying to will herself to simmer down, longing to get on the plane and relax with a drink. God, she needed it, she thought, her nerves felt like the teeth of a saw, cutting their way into her brain.

And when she reached the desk she was told there was a delay, so instead she went to stand in line at the self-service counter and eventually managed to get a coffee and a sandwich, but then had to stand up to eat them because all the seats round the tables were taken; not that Cassie particularly wanted to sit down when she saw the white plastic tables piled with dirty crockery, their surfaces unwiped and wet with spilt drinks. After half an hour she went back to the desk and demanded to know what was happening.

'I'm sorry, madam,' the receptionist told her, 'but all flights to Scotland have been grounded indefinitely because of freezing fog that's come down in the Glasgow and Edinburgh area.'

'Indefinitely?' Cassie stared at the man in horror. 'But haven't you any idea how long it's going to be?'

'Sorry, we've just got to wait until the fog lifts.'

'But that might not be until tomorrow!'

'That's possible, quite likely even,' the man said with a shrug, then pointed out, 'But perhaps, if you don't want to wait, you might consider going by train? I could phone through and book you a seat on the night express to Glasgow if you like?'

Cassie hesitated only a moment; there was no way she wanted to go home and then come all the way out to the airport again tomorrow. 'Yes, all right, do that for me, would you? And book me a sleeper, please.'

The receptionist phoned through while Cassie thought miserably of the long journey ahead, but at least she'd be able to get some sleep on the way. But that, too, was to be denied her in this worst of all weeks.

'I'm sorry, Mrs Ventris, but all the sleepers have been taken, but I've managed to get you a first class seat. The train leaves at nine-thirty.'

'Thanks.' Cassie picked up her case again and walked out into the cold air to get a taxi to take her back into London.

She spent the hours on the train in reading a novel that she'd bought at the bookstall in the station. She had also had a meal in the restaurant there because there was no buffet car on the train, so at least she wasn't hungry, only extremely bored as the high-speed train scorched through the night, past towns whose inhabitants were snugly tucked up in bed or seated in front of the fire, watching television. Cassie pictured them in her imagination and heartily envied them, her only comfort that she would be with Simon in just a few more hours.

Towards midnight it grew colder, despite the heating, and when she lifted up the blind she saw that it was snowing, large driving flakes that pelted the windows of the swiftly moving train. They stopped only three times on the way up, at Birmingham, Manchester and Carlisle, close to the Scottish border. At the latter station Cassie got up to stretch her legs and noted gloomily that the snow was already quite deep, clinging to the roofs and blowing into drifts at every exposed corner. But at least there was no fog here, although that didn't necessarily mean that there wouldn't be any further north in Glasgow, of course, but Cassie lived in hope.

And she was right; there wasn't any fog when she finally arrived in Glasgow in the early hours of the morning, just snow, a blinding, raging blizzard of snow that had taken every taxi off the streets and left them white and deserted, so that it looked more like Moscow in the depths of winter than anything else. Cassie took one look at it and hurried back into the station to find a phone. First she tried the airport, only to be told that conditions in the north-west were even worse than in Glasgow and that nothing—planes or helicopters— would be taking off until the blizzard stopped. Next she tried to phone Simon, but had to go through the operator and there was a great deal of delay and wrong connections until she finally got through to him.

'Cassie?' he exclaimed in sleepy surprise when he

heard her voice, then, on a sharper note, 'What is it? What's happened?'

'The plane couldn't take off because there was fog in Glasgow, so I took a train,' she explained. 'But now there's snow here and I can't get out to the site.'

'Took a train? D'you mean to say you're in Glasgow?'

'Yes, of course. Where did you think I was?'

'Back home at the flat. The company's representative at Heathrow phoned me to say you wouldn't be arriving by plane, but I'd no idea you'd come up by train.'

'You weren't waiting up for me, then?' Cassie demanded, her mental picture of Simon pacing the floor with worry beginning to fragment.

'No, I was in bed.'

'In bed! While I was sitting up in that damn cold train for hours and hours? And now I'm stuck in this rotten station at three o'clock in the morning with a blizzard raging outside, and no planes and no taxis and nowhere to go!' Her voice rose in shrill anger. 'Added to which I'm not dressed for a damn blizzard and I'm freezing!' Which was an exaggeration, because she was wearing a brown padded cotton jacket over her tweed suit, but her feet in a pair of the latest high-heeled leather boots were definitely beginning to feel the cold, as were her hands and nose.

Simon, recognising the note of extreme tiredness and near-panic in her voice, was immediately soothing and businesslike. 'Exactly where are you?'

'I told you, in Glasgow Station, and there aren't any taxis and I . . .'

'Okay, so here's what you do,' Simon interrupted tersely. 'You go and find the waiting-room and stay there until someone comes for you. I'll phone the hotel that Mullaine's uses—the one we stayed in last time, remember?—and get them to send a car for you.'

'And what happens if I get attacked or mugged or something while I'm waiting?' she demanded indignantly.

Even over the miles of line she could hear the laughter in Simon's voice. 'Just turn round and tell them what you think of Scotland in general and Glasgow in particular; they'll soon turn round and run.'

'*Simon!*' But even through her indignation she saw the funny side of it and had to laugh. 'Oh, darling,' she sighed, 'I'm sorry, only it's been such a rotten night. What shall I do, try to get a helicopter later on this morning?'

'No, you sit tight at the hotel. I'll try and get to you.'

'All right. But do hurry, darling. I miss you.'

'Don't worry,' he answered softly. 'If there's any way of getting through this to you, I'll make it.'

But the wintry conditions decreed otherwise and, after several abortive and frustrating attempts to reach Glasgow, Simon had to give up.

'I'm sorry, love,' he told her over the phone late on Saturday night, when the storm had raged without letting up all day, 'but there's just no way I can make it. I've tried everything: the helicopter, a Range Rover with chains on the tyres, snow-ploughs, even a boat to take me by sea, but they either refuse to risk the weather or else get bogged down after only a couple of miles; even the snow-plough couldn't make it.' The annoyance at having to admit defeat was clear in his voice and Cassie could imagine how galling he must find it that he could have so many means of transport at his disposal and yet be thwarted by a simple snowstorm.

Cassie gave a sigh of pure frustration, 'Oh, Simon, just when *are* we going to get together?'

'Just as soon as I can make it. Do you think that being away from you isn't driving me to distraction, too? But at least we can talk on the phone.'

'We could have done that when I was at home in London,' Cassie pointed out acidly. 'I didn't come all this way just so that we could exchange platitudes over the phone.'

'But we're not going to just exchange platitudes.' His voice became soft, caressing. 'You're going to lie on your bed and I'm going to tell you exactly what I'm going to do to you the next time I make love to you. Now, lie back.'

Cassie smiled to herself and did as she was told, wriggling down deliciously on to the pillow and holding the receiver close to her ear. 'And just where do you propose to start?' she asked him huskily.

'At the top,' he told her, 'working my way slowly down with a couple of very interesting diversions to left and right on the way . . .'

Back in London, Cassie threw herself into her work with a rather grim determination to forget about Simon and being lonely. She tried to be philosophical about it, telling herself that other women, who were married to sailors, or soldiers, or something like that, were apart for far longer periods and managed to survive. The fact that the divorce rate among such couples was also very high, she could ignore; her's and Simon's feelings for each other were strong enough to weather even such a long separation as this. And gradually, as she again immersed herself in her work, to the exclusion of nearly everything else, it began to have an immunising effect, cushioning her from any real feelings, so that her frustration and loneliness were buried beneath constant activity, channelling all her energy into her work where before she divided it between work, home, friends and her social life.

At the beginning of April she went to Paris again for a big fashion fair showing all the new French and Italian ready-to-wear collections. It was exciting, it was fun, and Cassie came back full of ideas and plans that she was eager to work on and develop at home while they were fresh in her mind. But when she got back from the airport and went up to the flat, Simon opened the door for her before she even got her key out of her bag.

'Oh, it's you!' For a moment she was so taken aback at seeing him that she could only stare foolishly.

He laughed and bent down to pick up her case, then drew her inside and shut the door. 'Stop looking at me as if I were a ghost. I'm real.'

'Are you?' she asked huskily. 'I was beginning to wonder.'

'Well, in that case I'd better prove it to you.' He set down her case and moved purposefully forward, taking her in his arms to kiss her, slowly at first, his lips exploring hers gently, as if he was kissing her for the very first time, but then they grew harder, awakening a response so that she opened her mouth in surrender, giving herself wholly to his embrace.

When at last he lifted his head, Cassie looked up at him, her green eyes misty and languorous. Breathlessly she said, 'Now I know it's you. Only you could kiss like that.'

His eyebrows rose. 'Oh? And just who have you been

comparing me with?' he demanded.

Cassie laughed. 'Wouldn't you like to know?' Then
she began to fire questions at him as she unbuttoned
her coat and he helped her off with it. 'When did you
get home? How long can you stay? Have you worked
out the new pay policy? Have all the unions agreed?
Have you eaten yet? I'm starving,' she added as she
made for the kitchen and pulled open the door of the
fridge. 'Did Mrs Payne get the groceries I asked her
to? Let's cook some . . .'

She broke off as Simon caught hold of her shoulders
and turned her round to face him.

'Yesterday, till Monday, no, no, no, yes.'

Cassie looked at him in bewilderment. 'What did
you say?'

'I merely answered your questions. I got home yesterday; I can stay till Monday; no, the unions haven't
yet agreed to a pay policy; no, I haven't eaten, and yes,
Mrs Payne did get the groceries. Now, will you just
simmer down a minute and let me tell you something.'

'What? Is it important?' Cassie asked on a note of
alarm.

'Very important,' he agreed gravely, but then he
smiled as he put a hand on either side of her face and
said softly, 'I wanted to tell you that I've missed you, I
need you, and I love you—so very much.' Then he
kissed her again, long and lingeringly.

'Oh, Simon!' Cassie put her arms round his neck
and let him hold her close. 'It's been such a long time.'
She smiled at him. 'I was beginning to forget what it
was like to be married.'

Simon laughed with her as he let her go, but a faint
shadow came into his eyes as he watched her busy herself with the preparation of a meal. After a moment he

put out a hand to stop her. 'Tell you what, why don't I go out and get a Chinese meal?'

'Would you? That would be lovely; I didn't really feel like cooking.'

'Be back in about twenty minutes,' he promised as he kissed her on the nose before going to put on his overcoat.

But it was nearer half an hour before Simon returned, and then he was rather annoyed to find that Cassie was sitting at the table writing in a notebook and had made no attempt to set the table or put any plates to warm.

She looked up in some surprise as he walked in. 'Good heavens, are you back already? Sorry, I just sat down to make a note of some ideas I had on the way back from Paris and forgot the time.' She jumped up and began to get out the cutlery and mats. 'It won't take a minute.'

'How did you get on in Paris?' Simon called from the kitchen where he was plunging a couple of dinner plates in hot water to warm them.

'Oh, it was super. I think this was one of the most successful fashion fairs they've held.' She went on telling him about the trip as they ate, describing the new styles in detail, and enthusiastically outlining her own plans for displaying the goods in the various fashion departments at Marriott & Brown's.

Simon listened and asked several questions, but the warm, interested look in his eyes gradually faded and was replaced by a slight frown as he detected a harder note in Cassie's voice as she talked about a deal she'd pulled off, a slightly ruthless edge that had never been there before.

After the meal they sat together on the settee for a

while, listening to some new L.P.s that Simon had bought, his arm round her and Cassie's head on his shoulder. But after a while she began to fidget restlessly and then sat up. 'Shan't be a minute; I just want to make a note of an idea I have for the swimwear department.'

Picking up her notebook, she sat down at the table again and began to write hurriedly, her ideas coming too fast for her to write in anything neater than a hasty scrawl. When the record ended she was still writing and Simon got up and quietly turned it over. His eyes settled on her reflectively as he went back to his seat, realising that she was so immersed in what she was doing that she hadn't even noticed that the music had stopped.

An hour later he stood up abruptly, turned off the record player and came to take the pen from her hand. Cassie looked up, an indignant frown on her face, her mouth open to make a sharp objection, but then she realised who it was and she flushed guiltily.

'Oh, lor', I did it again, didn't I?' Contritely she closed the notebook and stood up. 'I'm sorry, darling. It's just that I'm so full of ideas after Paris, and I'm afraid that if I don't put them all down I'll forget them.'

She looked up at him, her green eyes wistful and pleading, and Simon found it impossible to be angry. He reached up to stroke the smooth, pale skin of her cheek and the harsh comment he had been about to make died in his throat. Instead he said thickly, 'Let's go to bed.'

Her face came alive with love and longing. 'Oh, yes— let's!'

They made love with a turbulent passion, each of

them satisfying their own needs greedily, but in so doing arousing the other's to new heights of sensuality—new and yet not new—for each of them knew the other's body as intimately as their own and was aware of what pleased and excited them the most. Simon had taught Cassie never to be shy or hold back, to tell him when something he did gave her enjoyment, until there was no longer any need to tell him and she could only moan, 'Yes—oh, Simon, yes!' as he brought her to one ecstatic climax after another.

They had been apart for a long time and it was late when Simon finally turned her on to her side and lay close beside her, his arm across her possessively, encompassing her with the protection of his body as he fell into a contented sleep.

Some slight noise woke him a couple of hours later and he stirred, then remembered where he was and reached out to put his arm round Cassie again. But she wasn't there, the bed was empty. He thought she must have gone to the bathroom, but the bathroom opened off the bedroom and there was no light under the door. Getting up, he slipped on a bathrobe and walked quietly down the corridor to the sitting-room. Cassie was sitting on the settee in the pool of light thrown by the standard lamp, her dressing grown wrapped round her and her feet tucked under her. She was busily writing in her notebook again. Simon watched her for a long moment, then turned and went silently back to the bedroom, to lie thoughtfully and smoke a cigarette as he waited for his wife to come back to bed.

'Cassie? It's John Russell.'

'Oh, hi, John. How are you?'

It was a Saturday afternoon, the weekend after

Simon had managed to get home, and Cassie had been washing her hair when the phone rang.

'I'm fine. You?'

'Yes, great.'

'Good. I was afraid I wouldn't catch you, that you would already have set out to meet Julia.'

'Julia?' Cassie queried on a note of surprise.

'Yes. Look, she's gone out without her chequebook and credit cards—I've just found her wallet on the hall table.' He chuckled. 'She'll be mad as fire when she goes to buy something and finds she can't!'

'Well, I don't suppose *you're* altogether sorry,' Cassie returned, jokingly. 'But look, John, you've got it wrong, I haven't . . .'

She was going to add that she hadn't made any arrangement to meet Julia that day, but he interrupted her by saying, 'Must rush, I've got a golf match this afternoon. But she said she was going out with you, so I thought I'd better let you know in case she started panicking and reported the wallet stolen or something. You know what she's like,' he added with all the husbandly lack of sympathy that comes after a ten-year marriage.

'But, John . . .'

'Must go, love. See you.'

And he put the phone down before she could protest any further. Cassie shrugged as she replaced her own receiver; obviously he'd got her mixed up with some other friend that Julia was going shopping with, although he'd seemed pretty definite about it. And, come to think of it, Julia had never mentioned having shopping trips in the West End with anyone else, often saying that she liked to go with Cassie because she had such a good fashion sense. Well, whoever she was with she wouldn't be buying much today without her money.

It was only later, when Cassie was blow-drying her hair and reading a magazine at the same time, that her eye chanced on a letter to the agony column in which a married woman who was having an affair asked for advice, and it occurred to her to wonder if Julia had been using her as an excuse and that she might be meeting another man. At first she dismissed the idea as ludicrous. Julia just wasn't the type, and besides, she loved her home and family too much. But then Cassie remembered uneasily that Julia hadn't phoned her to go out on a Saturday for several weeks, and that the last time she had seen her she'd been more than a little fed up with John and his incessant golf. The more she thought about it, the more worried she became. One read so often of people having affairs that it had become commonplace, but the thought that it was someone you knew quite well made the whole idea shocking and wrong. Cassie decided in the end to phone Julia as if nothing had happened and suggest they meet and then try to find out if she was right. She didn't want to do it, it was like peeping through bedroom keyholes, but she felt that she had a right to know if Julia was using her as an excuse to meet a lover. And besides, she might easily have given the game away to John, and the last thing she wanted was to be involved in a marital row.

But as it happened any approach she might make was forestalled, because Julia phoned her at work on the Monday morning and asked her to have lunch with her. Almost as soon as they met, Cassie knew that she had been right. There was a slightly ashamed, obstinate look in her friend's eyes, but apart from that she looked radiant. She had always been smart and had kept her figure in good shape, despite having had two children close together, but now there was a snap in her walk and she carried herself with a confident air, her head high, and she looked young and happy.

They sat down at a table in a small French restaurant behind Oxford Street and Cassie looked at Julia in surprise and perturbation. They gave their order and then Julia looked across at her and flushed.

'I suppose I don't have to tell you. You've already guessed, I can see it in your face.'

Cassie nodded, unable to speak, then burst out, 'Julia, how could you?'

Julia's flush deepened and she looked down at the table, then shrugged defensively. 'It just—happened.'

'Oh, rubbish!' Cassie returned, angry now. 'Don't try and fool me, Julia, things like that don't just happen. There has to be a moment when you either commit yourself or draw back. You've gone into this with your eyes open and it's no use pretending otherwise, even to yourself.'

'Well, all right. But I don't know what you're getting so upset about,' Julia retorted, the flush on her face giving way to anger.

'Because I like John, of course. I like you both. For heaven's sake, Julia, you're my *friends*!'

For a moment they fell into an awkward silence, prolonged as the waiter brought their first course. They ate without speaking, neither of them knowing quite what to say, until Cassie said impulsively, 'I just don't understand how you could do this to John. I thought you loved him.'

'But I do love him.'

'Then *why*, Julia? What has he done to make you

cheat on him with another man?'

Julia's reply was heavy with cynicism. 'Nothing— that's the whole point.'

Cassie shook her head. 'I'm sorry, I don't understand.'

Julia pushed her plate away and leant forward. 'Cassie, John and I have been married for over ten years. I loved him when we married and I still do, but he's changed. All he seems to think about now is the office and golf. Oh, he loves the kids, of course he does, and he gives them time during the school holidays—in fact he has more time for them than he does me,' she added bitterly. 'And he never seems to want to go out socially any more, unless it's to a golf club function.' She paused for a moment, her hands gripping each other on the table. 'We still make love, if you can call a quick five minutes once or twice a week making love. But I don't get anything out of it. As a matter of fact I never have; John was never very good at it. But that didn't used to matter, because I loved him and because he was attentive and caring in other ways. But now he isn't, and there's only so much pretending one can do, so much indifference one can take . . .'

She broke off, her voice unsteady, while Cassie looked at her in horror. Impulsively she put out a hand to cover her friend's. 'Oh, Julia, I'm sorry. I didn't know, I had no idea. You always seemed so happy together.'

Julia sat up and shrugged. 'I suppose we are, really, as far as most marriages go. John's quite happy, at any rate. But for a long time I've felt that I'm missing out on life. That I'm only thirty-one years old but that I've already settled into the pattern that I'll be in for the rest of my life. That was until I met . . .'

She hesitated and Cassie said swiftly, 'I don't want to know who it is. Please don't tell me, Julia.'

'No,' her friend answered slowly, 'maybe it's better if you don't know. Anyway, when I met him my life changed completely. I felt young and attractive again. Can you guess what it's like, Cassie, to find yourself wanted again, to have a man find you so desirable that he's crazy to go to bed with you?'

'But surely other men have found you attractive, too? I've seen you flirt at parties before and . . .'

'Oh, harmless suburban party flirtations—just a couple of kisses and a quick grope when you've both had enough drinks not to care what you're doing. That's almost de rigueur,' Julia declared scathingly. 'No, this is real, Cassie. He started chasing me the day after we met and wouldn't take no for an answer until we'd slept together. And it's wonderful, Cassie, it really is. For the first time I'm getting something out of sex, as well as giving. And he's so young and strong.' Her eyes sparkled with remembrance. 'Sometimes we make love all afternoon until it's so late that I just have to go home, and even then he doesn't want to stop.'

Cassie looked away, embarrassed at hearing such bedroom secrets, and yet no longer able to condemn her friend completely. At length, when Julia fell silent, Cassie said with difficulty, 'Are you going to leave John?'

'Oh, no! No, of course not.' Julia's answer was swift and certain. 'I know that this can't last, that it's nothing but sex and will eventually burn itself out. And, as I said, I love John and don't want to hurt him. And you know, Cassie, it's the strangest thing, but somehow, having this affair has made me appreciate John more. I know that sounds crazy, but it's true. And when it's over and I have to settle back into my old familiar rut again—well, at least I'll have this to look back on and remember.'

Seeing the sparkle in her friend's eyes, the glow in her face, Cassie could only look at her in wonder. Could just pure sex, sex without love, have such an effect? And would Julia be content to just return to her old life when the affair ended? Somehow Cassie couldn't believe that it would be that simple. There was always the risk that John would find out, as he almost had yesterday. And perhaps, even if this affair did end amicably, Julia might again become dissatisfied later on and look round for another man. If she could get away with having an affair successfully once, why not twice, or three times?

Deliberately Cassie changed the subject, reluctant to pursue her thoughts further, and luckily Julia refrained from saying anything else, although it was clear that she was disappointed, that she would dearly have loved to talk about her new found happiness. So neither of them mentioned it again until they were standing outside the restaurant on the pavement, under a thin April sunshine. Then Julia said, 'It will be all right to tell John I'm going shopping with you again next Saturday afternoon, won't it?'

With difficulty, Cassie answered, 'I'm sorry, Julia, I'd rather you didn't.'

'But why? I thought you were my friend.'

'I hope I am. And if it was just you perhaps then I'd say yes. But John's a friend as well, and I couldn't lie to him—I don't want to *have* to lie to him.'

'I see.' There was a reproach in Julia's tone that made Cassie almost change her mind, because she was quite sure that their friendship would never be the same again, but she stayed silent. 'Well, I'll just have to think of some other excuse, won't I? Not that it matters; I find that you can always think of a thousand excuses if you want something badly enough.'

Cassie looked at her defiant face and said sadly, 'A thousand lies, you mean.'

For a moment the older girl glared at her angrily, then she seemed to crumple, her shoulders sagging. 'I can't help it, Cassie. I need him so badly, you see.' Then she hurriedly turned away and walked quickly down the street.

Cassie watched her go and, not for the first time in her marriage, thanked her stars that Simon was an ardent, virile lover.

CHAPTER FIVE

It was several weeks before Cassie began to fully realise that not only the work and home pattern of her life,
but also the social one, was changing. She and Simon
had entertained quite a lot and been asked out in
return, and they often went to parties and discos, less
often to night clubs, but always with some of their
contemporaries. They also had various friends, couples
they would make up a four or six with to go to the
theatre and ballet, both of which Cassie thoroughly
enjoyed. But now that Simon was in Scotland she
found that the social invitations had come to an abrupt
stop. At first her new responsibilities had kept her too
busy to take much notice, but when she ran into a
couple of friends in the local supermarket one
Saturday, she gathered from the gossip that several
things had taken place among the crowd she usually
mixed with to which she hadn't been invited.

Her first feelings were of indignation and resentment, but when she thought about it rationally she
realised that an odd woman stood out at most gather-
ings like a sore thumb. Since her marriage—no, before
that even—since she had first started dating steadily
with Simon, all their social life had been with other
couples, and she felt a pang of guilt when she thought
of all the not-so-lucky girl friends that she used to go
around with that she had almost immediately dropped.
Now most of them had dropped from sight completely,
and the two or three others she met perhaps once a

year or just exchanged a letter with the annual Christmas card. And Cassie could understand why she wasn't invited along by the usual crowd; there were far too many single girls or divorced women in London already, looking for a man, and not loath to look at someone else's if they couldn't find one that wasn't attached. And with a jolt Cassie realised that that was virtually what she was now; a single girl during the week and a wife on the few weekends that her husband could get home and claim his rights, she thought cynically.

Deciding that she wasn't going to sit back and passively let her social life die, she made the effort to get herself tickets for a ballet she had wanted to see and for the new play at the National Theatre, but although she enjoyed the evenings, it just wasn't the same without Simon. The disruption of her home life, even an intermittent sex-life, she could stand, but the fact that her social life was going to be virtually non-existent for three years nagged at her constantly, especially when she *did* get invitations which she had to turn down virtually at the last minute as she hoped that Simon would get home but then he couldn't make it. One or two of the people were annoyed, and Cassie didn't blame them; she would be annoyed herself if one of her dinner parties was spoilt at the last minute, and she knew it was unlikely that the people would invite them again while Simon was in Scotland.

Her phone calls to Simon started to become less than loverlike as she demanded to know *exactly* when he was coming home.

'I've told you, darling,' he would explain patiently, 'most of the stuff has to be brought in by sea, and the gales over the North Sea for the past month have delayed everything.'

'There aren't any gales now,' Cassie pointed out irascibly.

'No, which is why everyone's working flat out to get the ships unloaded and to get back on schedule.'

'Can't you at least get Easter off?'

'I'm afraid not, everyone's working seven days a week at the moment.'

'But you don't have to, surely? You're the boss, Simon, you're supposed to delegate, for God's sake!'

His voice grew cold. 'This is my baby, Cassie. I've taken the job on and I have to be on hand to see it through its teething troubles before I can take any length of time off.'

'Oh, for heaven's sake. Your baby!' Her tone sharpened with sarcasm. 'Anyone would think it was a real baby, the way you fuss over that site!'

Even over the phone Cassie could hear the withdrawal in his voice as he answered, 'I wouldn't know about that.'

'And what's that supposed to mean?' she snapped.

'It doesn't mean anything. Stop trying to pick a fight.'

'I am not trying to pick a fight. I'm . . .'

'No?' His voice was sneering. 'You're certainly giving a good imitation, then.'

'As I was saying,' Cassie went on through gritted teeth, 'I'm merely trying to find out if there is any possibility whatsoever of us having even a semblance of a social life. Do I accept this invitation to Anne and David's party or not?'

Simon sighed. 'I've already told you, love, I just can't leave here at the moment. Look, why don't you come up this weekend and I'll meet you in Glasgow and we'll . . .'

'No, I won't,' Cassie retorted angrily. 'I've seen enough of Glasgow hotel rooms to last me for a lifetime. If it's too much effort for you to try and get home, then why the hell should I bother?' And she slammed down the phone.

It rang again almost immediately and she sat looking at it resentfully, seething with anger, knowing it was Simon and determined not to answer it. But the strident rings kept on and on and eventually she shot out her hand and picked it up.

'Well?' she demanded belligerently.

'Hey, we're both in the same union, remember?' Simon's voice said softly, forcefully, and suddenly her temper was gone, the anger disappeared.

'Oh, Simon, what an idiot thing to say!' And she laughed despite herself.

'But true,' he insisted.

Cassie was silent for a long moment, then said, 'I'm sorry. I was beastly, wasn't I?'

He laughed, his voice back to normal. 'A temper is to be expected along with green eyes and chestnut hair.'

She wrinkled her nose. 'I do try not to lose it.'

'I know.' He paused, then added, 'You want to have it both ways, Cassie; to keep your job and to have me with you, but you've got to realise that you can't have both. I'll get home when I can, you know that.'

'That sounds a very reasonable attitude,' Cassie answered, her voice prickly again.

'But you don't feel reasonable?'

'No, I feel randy.'

Simon gave a laugh that was half a groan. 'When

you say things like that you tempt me to just throw up everything and take the first plane home.'

'Then do it,' Cassie pleaded urgently. 'Come home and take me to bed, darling. I'm tired of conducting my sex life at the end of a telephone line.'

He groaned again. 'Cassie, for God's sake! Do you think I don't want to?'

'But you won't?' she said flatly, dully.

'I can't.'

She was silent for a long moment, then merely said bleakly, 'Goodnight, Simon,' and put the phone down again before he had time to say anything more than her name in protest.

He didn't phone back a second time. Cassie half hoped he would, but they both knew that it wouldn't do any good, they would only tear into each other again, widen the gap that was beginning to open between them.

During the next few weeks Cassie felt as if she was on a roller-coaster; the weekdays were the downhill parts where everything happened very fast and the adrenalin flowed like mad, and the evenings and weekends were the everlastingly slow, dragging climbs up to the next peak of activity. She didn't see Julia at all for shopping trips now, but once or twice she spent Saturday afternoons with Sue Martin, whose husband was still busy doing extra work for his company, and they drew some comfort from being able to commiserate with one another and grumble about their husbands' jobs.

One Friday evening, with only an empty weekend ahead, to cheer herself up Cassie tried on a new outfit that she'd bought on her staff discount in the store. It was the new buccaneer look with soft wine velvet knickerbockers, a white blouse with lots of cascading lace at the front and on the cuffs, and a beaded sash which she put across her shoulder and knotted at the waist. To amuse herself she tried out a different way of doing her face, using more colourful and rather bizarre make-up. Her hair she tonged into tightish waves at the ends, and then pulled back from her head on one side, clipping it in place with a big ornamental hairslide with a colourful butterfly on it. Then she sprayed on some of the French perfume that she'd brought back on her last trip to Paris and stood back to study the effect in the mirror.

At first she looked at herself with the critical eye of a fashion buyer. This was the image that she had decided to promote in the Top Togs department for this season, and already it was beginning to catch on. But the important part was how it was put together, every accessory to give the complete look had to be available in the store so that the average girl would be able to picture herself in the outfit and buy everything there and then while she was still full of enthusiasm. A buyer had to decide on what her fashion statement for that season was going to be in each particular department and then had to be careful not to go outside the season's image.

Then she looked at her reflection, knowing that the clothes weren't really her scene, but seeing that she looked attractive in them and thinking of the way Simon would have reacted, raising his eyebrows and laughing at her, but liking the change all the same. And he would have taken her out to a disco somewhere, probably one of the 'in' places in the West End, happy to show her off, his eyes proud as he looked at her, and then he would have taken her home and carried her into the bedroom, and said, 'Now, *this* is what I do to pirates.'

Abruptly Cassie turned away from the mirror and strode into the sitting-room. What the hell was the use in having new clothes if there was no one to see them? She was too young and full of life and energy to just sit at home alone every night. She poured herself a drink and took a long gulp of it, then picked up the phone and searched through her address book until she found the number of one of her single girl friends. Several phone calls later she put down the receiver and bit her lip, close to tears of frustration; either there had been no reply, or the girls already had dates, or they were washing their hair in readiness for a date tomorrow. Cassie suddenly felt more lonely than she had ever been in her life, and she took another long swallow of her drink. It was too late now to go to the cinema, too late to do anything except go to the pub for a drink or to a restaurant for a solitary meal. But she'd already eaten, and, even in this enlightened day and age, she didn't care to go and sit in a bar on her own. For a moment she contemplated going to visit her parents for the weekend, but couldn't stand the thought of her mother's inevitable cross-examination. So all that was left was another evening alone watching television or listening to music. Miserably Cassie poured herself another drink and turned on the set just as the doorbell rang.

The man standing in the hallway was a stranger. He was about thirty and tall, almost as tall as Simon, with thick dark blond curly hair and one of those moustaches that came down on either side of his top lip. He had a deep suntan that made his hair look lighter and pale blue eyes that widened appreciatively when he looked her over. He lifted his broad shoulders from where he had been leaning against the wall and said in an American accent, 'Hi. You must be Cassie?'

'Why—why, yes.' She looked at him in surprise, wondering how he knew who she was. She'd certainly never met him before, she was sure of that; he was the type of man that if you'd met him you wouldn't forget.

He grinned. 'It's okay, you don't know me. The name's Tom Rydell. Simon and I worked together a few years back, and he told me to look him up whenever I was in London.'

'Oh. Well—er—how do you do.' Cassie's hand was taken in a strong grip that hurt her fingers. 'You'd better come in.'

She led the way into the sitting-room and then turned to look at her visitor. 'Can I get you a drink, Mr Rydell?'

'Sure, Scotch on the rocks would be fine. And I said my name was Tom.'

Cassie smiled at him, liking his open friendliness. 'All right—Tom.'

She gave him his drink and gestured to a chair. 'Do sit down.' She sat opposite him and said, 'I'm afraid Simon isn't here. Mullaine's have put him in charge of an oil terminal they're building in Scotland and Simon is living up there until the job's finished.'

'Hey, that's too bad. I was really looking forward to seeing him again and rehashing the old days over a few beers. But maybe I'll be able to get up to Scotland to see him.'

'I'm sure he'll be pleased if you could. Where did you work with Simon?'

'Over in the States. He was over there for six months in the New York office of Mullaine's.'

'Yes, that's right. But that was before I met him.'

'Yeah, but we kept in touch for a while. He even sent me an invitation to your wedding, but I couldn't make it because by then I'd left Mullaine's and decided to go it alone.'

'You mean you started up your own company? That was very enterprising of you. How's it going?'

He gave her a wide grin, showing white, even teeth. 'Just great. As a matter of fact I'm over here to open up a London branch.'

He talked for a while about his company, then said, 'But how about you? Why aren't you with Simon in Scotland?'

His eyes ran over her again as he spoke, openly liking what he saw, and Cassie reacted instinctively to his admiration, putting up a hand to her hair and sitting up a little straighter so that the material of her blouse tightened across her breasts. 'Oh, I have my own career.'

She told him about it and then suggested she phone Simon so that they could at least speak to each other. Tom thought it a great idea, and the two men talked for quite some time while Cassie sat quietly in a chair with a magazine, pretending not to listen to Tom's half of the conversation. It appeared that the two of them had had quite some times together in New York, and she made a mental note to ask Simon one or two pointed questions next time she saw him—*when* she saw him.

Tom was still chuckling as he put down the phone. 'Say, it's a real shame Simon isn't here. I was kind of depending on him to show me my way around London.'

'Haven't you been here before?'

'No, it's my first trip.'

'Would you like another drink?' Cassie got up to get his glass.

'Well, thanks, but . . .' He looked up at her as she reached out a hand to take it. 'Hey, were you going out or something before I called? I'm not keeping you, am I?'

Cassie smiled slightly. 'No, I wasn't going out.'

'Then,' he hesitated, 'how about you coming out with me for a drink? I don't know any places in London and I'd sure be grateful if you could show me round a little,' he added with a grin. .

Cassie, too, hesitated, but only for a moment, then she tossed her hair back and said, 'Okay, why not?' She smiled back at him; that grin was infectious.

She guessed that he'd like some typical English atmosphere, so took him to an old-fashioned pub near Highgate Hill before going on to one of the new discos in the West End. Then, nearer breakfast than supper time, they went on to a salt-beef bar and watched the assistant expertly carve thick slices from a huge roast of meat, brown at the edges but still pink in the middle, and place them between two slices of crisp white bread. They munched the delicious sandwiches, talking as they ate; they hardly seemed to have stopped talking since the moment they met.

By the time she got home at about four in the morning, Cassie felt like a different person, the boredom and frustration was gone and she felt young and alive again. It had been fun to show her kind of London to someone new, to someone who appreciated and enjoyed the places she took him. And, she had to admit it, it had been a great boost to her ego to have an escort as good-looking as Tom, to have other girls watching and envying her. Especially when she could be completely at ease with Tom because he was just a friend, there were none of the nerves she'd felt when she'd been single and had gone out with a new boy-friend for the first time: would he ask her out again, would he try and proposition her or take her back to his place? Until she had met Simon it had always been like that, but it was amazing how quickly she'd forgotten, how glad she was that she didn't have to go through it again. Tom saw her safely into the flat and somehow, despite her weak protests, she found herself promising to take him on a sightseeing tour round London the next day.

From then on life became full and hectic again, with Tom monopolising every minute of her spare time. At first she tried to make a determined effort to protest about him wasting his time with her when he could be escorting more eligible girls, and offered to introduce him to one of her unattached friends, but he laughed the idea away.

'Aren't you enjoying showing me around, Cassie?'

'Well, of course I am, but . . .'

'Then why try to push me off on one of your girl friends?'

'I'm not trying to push you off, it's just that . . . well, I'm married to Simon and you're free, and you might want—er—might want to have more from—er—a relationship than I—er . . .' She stopped, floundering and then realised that Tom was openly laughing at her. She flushed and gave him a mock punch in the ribs. 'Oh, hell, you *know* what I mean.'

They had been walking along the street, but now Tom stopped and pulled her arm through his. 'Hey, you blushed!'

'No, I didn't,' Cassie denied, her cheeks flaming more than ever.

Tom put a finger up to touch her face. 'Sure you did. Say, you English girls are really something. I haven't met a girl who blushed in years.'

'Well, if you like English girls why don't you let me introduce you to . . .'

He moved his finger to put it over her lips. 'I like *you*. Why should I take a chance on dating some strange girl when I already have the prettiest one in town to show me around?'

'Oh, but . . .'

'No buts. And I know what you're thinking, but I'm quite capable of taking care of my own sex life. Okay?'

Cassie looked up into his amused blue eyes, found herself starting to blush again and hastily looked away. 'Okay.'

'Now,' he kept a firm hold on her arm, 'didn't you promise me a ride on top of one of your London buses?'

From that moment on their friendship altered subtly, became at once both easier and yet more binding. Cassie didn't again suggest that he date another girl, and she didn't draw away when he kept hold of her hand after helping her down some steps or across the street, or when he gave her a friendly kiss of greeting or farewell. And being American, he was very solicitous, making sure she was always comfortable and had everything she wanted, buying her small, crazy surprise presents as well as the flowers that he always brought whenever he called at the flat to pick her up. And Cassie sparkled under his attentions, loving being made such a fuss of, especially as there were no strings, knowing that he valued her for her friendship. It was a heady feeling, like old wine.

Simon was still battling with his problems in

Scotland; several times Cassie came home late from an evening spent with Tom after he'd picked her up straight from work, and found that Simon had left a message on the answer-phone for her. She had told him, of course, that she was showing Tom round London, but that was at the beginning and since then she had played it down, knowing that there was no harm in her going out with Tom for the couple of weeks he was to be in England, but afraid that Simon wouldn't see it the same way.

Only Tom showed no sign of hurrying back to America. He had found premises for his new branch quite quickly and had ordered all the necessary equipment: computer, telex, word processor, that kind of thing, and had placed ads for staff in the London area papers. That he was a dynamic businessman behind his lazy grin and casual air, Cassie found out almost at once when she went with him to an estate agent's office and they attempted to keep him waiting for someone they thought would be a more financially rewarding client. Tom didn't say much, but what he did say made the red-faced estate agent give him his immediate and undivided attention. So she knew that he could get things moving when he wanted to, but now he showed no signs of hurry, taking his time in interviewing staff and driving all over the place to follow up contacts and leads for new business.

Cassie saw him nearly every night now as a matter of course, and she no longer suggested somewhere for them to go; Tom had quickly got to know London and now took her to places she would never have dreamt of going with Simon, such as to watch greyhound racing, Japanese wrestling, or to an open-air jazz concert in the grounds of a mansion in Hertfordshire. During the latter they had shared a bottle of champagne and were merry and laughing on the way back in the car that Tom had hired. Tom was singing old Colonial songs and making Cassie join in the choruses even though she protested that she couldn't sing, so that she was still gurgling with laughter as she let herself into the flat.

Tom followed her in. 'You okay now?'

'Mm, fine.' Cassie turned to face him. 'Goodnight, Tom. Thanks for a great evening.'

'My pleasure.' He bent to kiss her goodbye and Cassie giggled and put a hand up to rub her mouth. 'What is it?'

'It's your moustache, it tickles.'

He laughed and put his hands on her arms, holding her. 'It does, huh? Now I know how to get at you, then.' And he teasingly bent to try and kiss her again while Cassie laughingly pulled away. Only his hands were holding her so firmly that she couldn't move and had to submit to his teasing. She wasn't quite sure how or when it happened; one minute they were both laughing and she was struggling to get free, the next his hands on her arms were tightening, hurting her and the laughter had gone from his face, to be replaced by a look of intense desire. And then his lips were on hers, not friendly or teasing anymore, but filled with a passionate hunger as his mouth pressed against hers, hard and insistent, demanding that she open her lips and yield her mouth to the hot importunities of his.

For a few brief minutes, Cassie submitted before jerking her head away and saying sharply, 'No! Tom, don't.'

Immediately he lifted his head, but his fingers still bit into her arms and his breathing was unsteady.

'You—you'd better go.'

'Cassie?' His voice still sounded thick as he put a hand up to her chin, made her turn and look at him. 'Look, I—I know I shouldn't have done that, but you're so darned lovely that I . . .' He broke off and ran a hand through his hair, pushing it back off his forehead, then stepped away from her. 'I know I shouldn't have done it. I'm sorry. But it just happened. You don't have to be afraid, I'm not going to make a pass. So don't think that anything's changed, okay?' He came near her again, raised his hand as if he was going to touch her but then shoved it in his pocket.

Cassie looked at him, her eyes troubled, knowing in her heart that it couldn't be the same again and yet willing to believe that he meant it because that was what she wanted, too.

'I'll pick you up tomorrow; we'll go for a drive in the country, right?'

'I—I don't know.'

'Honey, trust me.' He grinned at her. 'Just pals, huh?'

Cassie laughed and said in a mock Cockney accent, 'Right y'are then, me old mate.'

Tom's eyes widened and he gave a full masculine laugh of appreciation. 'You're crazy, do you know that? Beautiful but crazy.' He kissed her very lightly on the forehead. 'See you tomorrow.'

Cassie lay awake for some time that night, telling herself that Tom had just got a little carried away, that was all. That it was just a kiss, and what was one kiss nowadays? Why, if she'd been single she'd have thought nothing of it, would have been surprised, in fact, if Tom hadn't tried to make a pass. But even though she told herself that it was nothing, the fact remained that no other man had kissed her like that since her marriage, and she felt strangely guilty, knowing that she should have pulled away earlier, that she hadn't protested forcibly enough or said no, she wouldn't go out with him again. And yet, at the same time, the very fact that Tom obviously found her attractive and desired her was a heady excitement. Simon had been away for so long that she had begun to doubt her own power and looks, and it was intensely satisfying to have them reconfirmed by someone as good-looking and macho as Tom.

But even so the fact that it had happened at all frightened her, and she wished fervently that Simon would come home. It had been so long now, over two months since she had seen him. She remembered that it was his birthday next week; usually they went out to the theatre to celebrate, but this year they might as well be a million miles apart for all the chance there was of him coming home. Cassie stirred restlessly and thumped the pillow. For heaven's sake, it was only half a day's journey away, you'd think he'd be able to get home for his damn birthday! The thought gave her an idea; perhaps he could be *made* to come home.

The next morning she started phoning round their friends, inviting them to a party the following Saturday, Simon's birthday. Then came the more difficult part. She dialled the number in Scotland, imagining the numbers singing along the telephone wires, clicking into place and the phone ringing in the house by the sea. But it was the maid who answered and told her that Simon had gone into Kinray, so she had to leave a message for him to phone back. Tom called to collect her before he did so, however, and it wasn't until she got home that evening that they finally made contact.

'I phoned earlier,' Simon told her, 'but you were out. You seem to be out quite often lately.'

'Do I?'

Simon resisted the challenge in her voice and asked, 'Where were you, at your mother's?'

'No,' Cassie hesitated for the briefest second. 'I was with Tom. We went to see the Hell Fire Caves at High Wycombe.' She went on hurriedly, before he could speak, 'Simon, I've had a wonderful idea. Everyone's been asking me how you're getting on—all our friends, that is—and you haven't seen any of them for so long that I thought it would be great if we could get them all together at the same time, so I—well, I've arranged a party for next Saturday for your birthday. Don't you think that that's a great idea?' she added on a note of desperation.

Simon's voice sounded tired. 'Yes, darling, I do, but you *know* the situation I'm in here. All the negotiations are at a very delicate stage and I have to be on hand in case any problems crop up. If you'll just be patient until the new contracts are all agreed on, then I promise I'll take a couple of weeks off and we'll go away together somewhere.'

'Oh, and when do you think that will be?'

'If all goes well it could be at the end of this month.'

'*If* all goes well. *If* one of the unions doesn't decide that someone else is getting more than them. *If* . . .'

'Cassie, listen . . .' Simon broke in.

'No, you listen. I'm sick and tired of listening to your promises. It's been over two months now. I want you here for that party next Saturday. Do you understand, Simon? *I want you here!*'

There was a pause in which she could hear her own heart beating. She gripped the receiver until her knuckles showed white, striving to control the mixture of anger, fear and yearning that had gone into her demand.

'Cassie, has something happened?'

For a moment she was tempted to tell him about Tom, but what was there to tell, just a kiss that had gone a bit deeper, that was all. So she answered, 'No. I just want you to be here, that's all.'

His voice hardened. 'So you decided to pressgang me by arranging this party?'

'Call it that, if you like. If your head office sent for you, you'd be on the next plane,' she pointed out furiously. 'Well, now I'm sending for you. I want you here on Saturday, so just—just *be here!*' Then she slammed the phone down, afraid that she would break down and he would hear her.

During the rest of that week, Cassie saw Tom as often as before, and though at first she had been afraid he would follow up his pass, he made no attempt to do so, was just as friendly and attentive as he'd been before, so that she was able to relax in his company again. For a while she had been in two minds about inviting him to Simon's party, but now she did so, and he immediately offered to buy all the drink.

'Oh, but I couldn't let you do that,' Cassie protested.

'Why not? Call it my birthday present to Simon, if you like.'

And he overrode her objections, entering into the organisation of the party with enthusiasm and coming round on the Saturday afternoon to bring all the drink and staying to help her with the food.

'What time's Simon arriving?' he asked her when they had more or less finished and were having a well-earned cup of coffee.

'I'm not sure, it depends on when he can get away,' Cassie prevaricated. Actually she had only spoken to Simon once since she had issued her ultimatum. That had been on Thursday evening when he had phoned briefly to say that he would try to get home on Saturday but couldn't guarantee it or give a time. And that was it. He had then rung off, obviously still angry with her.

'I'm sure looking forward to seeing him again,' Tom remarked casually.

'Yes, I expect you'll have a lot to talk about,' Cassie answered absently, her mind still on Simon's abrupt telephone call. Tom said something else which she didn't catch. 'I'm sorry, what did you say?'

'I said that Simon was a lucky man.'

Cassie turned towards him and found that Tom was watching her.

'Lucky? Oh, why? Because he works for Mullaine's still?'

'No, because he has this,' he told her, putting out his hand in a sweeping gesture to take in the flat, 'and because he has you.'

Cassie shook her head and opened her mouth to protest, but before she could speak Tom went on, 'Of course I also think he's kind of crazy.'

'Why?'

'Because he's gone to Scotland and left you alone here.'

Cassie's face hardened. 'And just what's that supposed to mean?' She set down her cup and stood up angrily. 'Just because Simon's away it doesn't necessarily mean that I'm going to be unfaithful to him, you know.'

Tom, too, stood up and came over to her. 'Hey, simmer down! I didn't say it did.' He put his hands on her shoulders. 'I merely meant that any guy who can stay away from someone as beautiful as you for so long must be crazy, that's all.'

'Oh! I'm sorry, I suppose I must be a bit edgy.' Cassie became aware of his hands on her shoulders, of his closeness, and moved away. 'Giving parties always makes me nervous.'

Tom watched her for a minute as she fussed over the table, rearranging some of the dishes and straightening the serving spoons. 'I also think that you're not the kind of girl who likes being alone.'

Cassie turned to him, shaking her head and laughing. 'Oh, but that's where you're wrong; I'm very independent and self-sufficient.'

'On the surface, maybe.' He moved to her side, his blue eyes fixed on her face. 'But underneath I think you're as vulnerable as the next girl. You need a man around, Cassie, someone to take care of you.'

His eyes held hers as Cassie gazed back at him uncertainly, then she quickly turned her head and said, 'No. No, I don't. I'm quite content to be on my own while Simon's away.'

She changed the subject then, and Tom left soon after to go back to his hotel to change for the party, but when he had gone, as she was herself getting ready, Cassie looked at her reflection in the mirror and wondered why he'd said that. Was she vulnerable? She'd never thought so before. But then she had never been alone for any length of time before; she had lived with her parents right up until her marriage and since

then had only been by herself on the occasions when
Simon had been away on business for a few days at a
time. Never long enough for her to have to rely on her
own resources or to get lonely or bored. Is that what's
wrong with me? she wondered, her green eyes staring
back at her from the mirror shadowed by doubt. Am I
incapable of being alone? *Do* I need someone, a man,
to take care of me?

Then she made a face at herself in the mirror,
shrugging off the idea. Of course she didn't need
anyone, she could manage perfectly well by herself.
But even so the thought came to her that the first three
months without Simon had been almost unbearable,
so what would the rest of the three years be like?

The party was as successful as any party can be when
the guest of honour doesn't turn up. Everyone Cassie
had invited came and they all brought birthday presents for Simon. She told them all that he would be
there later on and concentrated on being the hostess.
Julia and John Russell were there, of course, Julia
looking young and sparkly and flirting openly with her
husband, teasing and laughing at him, so that John,
too, looked happier than he'd done for some time. At
first Cassie thought that this must be because Julia
had given up her affair with another man and turned
her attention back to John; but then she realised that it
was because the affair was still going on that Julia was
so vibrant and alive, and that some of her happiness
had rubbed off on to the husband who now looked at
her with such pride and pleasure. Cassie watched them
both and wondered how on earth John could be so
blind, so complacent.

Determinedly she switched her attention to the other
guests, putting on a happy face and trying to take their

sympathy, as the time went on and Simon still didn't show up, with as much bravado as she could muster.

'Never mind, Cassie, perhaps he got caught up in another strike at Heathrow, or something. I'm sure I saw something in the paper about some kind of disruption that was threatened there,' Sue Martin told her.

'Yes, I expect it's something like that,' Cassie agreed, but not really believing it. She poured Sue another drink and one for herself. Although they didn't know Simon particularly well, she had invited the Martins to the party because Sue had seemed so down lately; she looked a little happier tonight, with her husband by her side, but she still had a lost, almost frightened look behind the social smile. Chris, though, seemed to have changed since Cassie had last seen him, he appeared to be far more confident and self-assured; evidently his new responsibilities at work had been good for him.

Tom came up to Cassie then and demanded that she dance with him. Cassie took a long swallow of her drink and stopped thinking about Simon and gave herself over to just plain enjoying herself. The music was good, there was plenty of food and drink, her guests were having a good time to judge from the talk and laughter, and Tom was being as attentive, and looking at her with as much admiration as any girl could wish. So what the hell did it matter if her husband cared more about working out some damn pay scheme than coming home to his own birthday party! Cassie looked up at Tom and gave him a brilliant smile as she moved into his arms for a slow number.

He had a great sense of rhythm, moving to the music, taking her with him. Cassie could smell his aftershave. It was different from Simon's, he used a tangy-smell-ing one, whereas Tom's had a more subtle, musky aroma. He held her close, but not too close, his hands on her back, warm through the thin material of the black harem outfit she was wearing. The room was rather crowded and Cassie stumbled against him as someone knocked into her. Tom's hands tightened and she felt the hardness of his chest against her breasts. She muttered an apology and went to draw away, but he held her there and she felt his face against her hair. Quickly she looked up and found him gazing down at her. For a long moment their eyes met and held, then Tom smiled at her and she relaxed against him, gradually letting her arms move upwards until her hands were resting on his shoulders.

The record came to an end and someone put on an aggressive reggae disc, changing the mood of the party completely for a while. Afterwards Cassie was busy serving the hot moussaka she'd made for supper while the guests helped themselves to the French bread, salad and other cold dishes that she'd set out beforehand. There was also a birthday cake with thirty-three candles around it, but this she took back into the kitchen and pushed into a corner. For a minute she stood looking at it, her mouth set into a bitter line, but then Tom came in looking for clean glasses and she switched back into the party again.

It was nearly three before the first people began to leave. Cassie had expected John and Julia to be among the first to go, but Julia had explained that they'd got a baby-sitter who was willing to stay overnight and so they could stay out late for a change. John, though, had begun to wilt earlier, sitting down in an armchair to watch while Julia danced with Chris Martin or some other man, and looking more frequently at his watch, then muttering about the golf tournament he was to play tomorrow.

By four there were only half a dozen couples left. The music was low now and smoochy for fear of waking people in the other flats. John had gone to sleep in his chair and Chris was dividing his time between his wife and Julia and evidently enjoying himself. Tom had taken Cassie's hand an hour ago and they had been dancing together ever since, except when they stopped to drink or say goodbye to people who were leaving. And it had seemed natural, after the way they had danced before, for him to draw her to him, his arms round her, her head on his shoulder.

At five Cassie rather blearily made coffee and everyone sat around and talked for a while until three of the last couples left, leaving only John and Julia, Sue and Chris and Tom and herself. It was quite obvious that John wanted to leave, and Sue, too, looked as if she was going to fall asleep any minute, but Julia and Chris were both still full of life and drink, laughing and making outlandish suggestions about what they should do next.

'I don't want to go home,' Julia was protesting. 'We ought to do something to make this party really memorable. Something like—oh, I don't know—like driving the wrong way up Oxford Street or flying up to Scotland to see Simon.'

Her husband grunted scornfully. 'You'll only end up in a police station by driving the wrong way along a one-way street, and as for going up to Scotland—I've never heard anything so ridiculous!'

'All right, maybe it is ridiculous!' Julia turned on him in annoyance. 'But at least it's something alive, something exciting. But then what would *you* know about life or excitement?' she added pettishly. 'All you ever think about is the office or golf. Anyone would think you were sixty instead of forty!'

There was a short, awkward silence, the kind there always is when outsiders get involved in a married couple's quarrel. Cassie looked away in embarrassment and saw that Sue was doing the same, but she noticed that Chris was looking openly at Julia with a small, amused smile on his lips. Even as Cassie began to wonder how on earth he could find amusement in someone else's marital scrap, she saw Julia turn her back on John and smile at Chris, a slow, secret smile of knowledge and understanding.

Cassie drew in her breath sharply, realising all too clearly just who Julia's lover was. A sound of protest came to her lips, but before she could utter it, Tom broke into the silence by saying, 'Hey, if we want to keep the party going, how's this for an idea? It's almost six o'clock; why don't we all go to the Savoy and have an early breakfast?'

Immediately Julia was all excitement again. 'Why, yes, that's a wonderful idea. Don't you think so, Chris?'

'Yes, sounds great,' he agreed. 'How about you, Cassie?'

For a moment she hesitated, but Cassie had no wish to end the party, to be alone in the empty flat with an uncut birthday cake, so she said with almost as much enthusiasm, 'Yes, I'd like to. It will be fun.'

'I'll need to freshen up first, though,' Julia said, and went off to the bedroom. John followed her and Sue determinedly drew Chris into the kitchen and shut the door, presumably to remonstrate with him if the sound of their raised voices was anything to go by.

Cassie walked over to the window, feeling suddenly depressed by what she had seen and by Simon's non-arrival. She reached up and drew the curtains, letting in the pale sunlight. It was the middle of June now, well into the spring, and it looked as if it was going to be a lovely day. Tom came up behind her, put his hands on her shoulders, then turned her slowly to face him.

'Cassie,' he murmured, his eyes exploring each feature of her face. 'I don't think I've ever seen you look lovelier than at this moment, with the light behind you, creating a halo round your head.'

His fingers tightened on her shoulders and he drew her slowly towards him. Desire flamed in his eyes and Cassie knew that he was going to kiss her. She was filled, suddenly, with a strong blaze of intense sexual awareness. She knew that she ought to move away, to speak, to do something that would break the spell, but she felt mesmerised and powerless to move, as if all her will-power had drained away. Her lips parted and she lifted her head to meet his.

'Cassie!'

They both turned, startled, to see Simon standing in the doorway, a look of murderous anger on his face.

CHAPTER SIX

FOR a few seconds Cassie was too paralysed by shock to move. She hadn't heard his key in the door, hadn't heard his steps in the hall. She felt Tom give a jerk of surprise, then he quickly took his hands from her shoulders and turned to face Simon. He started to say something, but Simon was already striding across the room, his hands doubled into tight fists, his mouth set into a snarl of determination and the look of savage rage still in his eyes.

Realisation of what he was about to do made her gasp with horror, but there was no time to do more than say his name before he was across the room and had grabbed Tom's lapel, raising his other fist to smash it into his face. Tom started to raise his arms in self-defence, but he had been taken by surprise and wouldn't have stood a chance. Then the bedroom door opened and Julia exclaimed, 'Simon! So you did make it after all? How lovely!'

A look of total astonishment came into Simon's furious grey eyes and he hesitated for a second, his arm still drawn back, and Tom had time to grab his fist before he could thrust it forward with all the force of his arm.

'Hi, old buddy. How are you?' Tom pulled his hand down and shook it as Julia came up to greet him followed by her husband. Then Sue and Chris, hearing the noise, came out of the kitchen and everyone seemed to be talking at once.

Cassie moved away, her legs feeling suddenly weak and trembly. Tom looked at her quickly, but she avoided his eyes. Behind her she could hear Simon saying that he couldn't get down by air so had travelled on the overnight train. They were all commiserating with him on having missed the party and he was agreeing, saying he was sorry he hadn't been able to make it earlier. He sounded so offhand about it that Cassie turned angrily on her heel and walked into the bedroom. Jerking open the wardrobe door, she yanked out a black evening jacket, pulling it out so roughly that the hanger fell off the rail. There was a mirror on the wardrobe door and in it she saw that Simon had followed her into the bedroom. Renewed anger filled her at his casual attitude, of the way he'd gone for Tom for no reason at all.

He came towards her, his face somewhat guarded. 'Aren't you even going to say hello to me?'

Cassie made no move to go to him, instead looked at him coldly and said, 'Hello, Simon. I suppose I ought to wish you many happy returns of yesterday. Only you *didn't* return yesterday, did you?'

She went to walk past him, but he caught her arm and stopped her. 'Cassie, wait.'

With a jerk of her arm she shook off his hand. 'Sorry,' she retorted acidly, 'but I've waited long enough.'

An exasperated frown drew his brows together. He began to say something, but Cassie ignored him and walked back into the sitting-room. The others were ready to leave and Tom silently took Cassie's jacket from her and held it while she put it on. She didn't look at him and he didn't touch her, but both of them were intensely aware of each other.

'Where are you off to?' Simon had come into the room and was watching them, the frown still between his eyes.

'We're rounding off the evening by having breakfast at the Savoy,' Julia told him with a laugh. 'You are going to come with us, aren't you? After all, it was your party.'

But before Simon could answer, Cassie put in, 'Oh, but you must remember, Julia, that Simon will be tired after his mad rush to try and get here. And if he's hungry,' she added shrewishly, 'he can always eat his birthday cake!'

She glared across at Simon as she spoke and saw the frown give way to a cold, remote look. She had seen that expression on his face before, but not often; it meant that he had drawn his emotions within himself, was holding them under a tight control until the right moment came to give them full rein, whether they were of love or anger. Only there was no doubt now which one he was feeling.

'On the contrary,' he answered with cool self-possession, completely ignoring Cassie's sarcasm and the surprised looks it had brought from the others, 'I shall be happy to come with you.'

'In that case,' Tom said easily, 'I'll be pushing along. I'll give you a call later this evening.'

He moved to go towards the door, but Cassie caught his arm. 'No, you must come with us. At least *you* bothered to come to the party; why should you have to leave before it's completely over?'

Tom looked slightly taken aback and the others uncomfortable, but Simon immediately said, 'Yes, Tom, you must come with us. We're not going to take no for an answer, especially when we haven't seen each other for so long.'

So Tom had no choice but to agree, and they all piled into his large car, Cassie working it so that she sat in the back between Chris and John who each had their wives on their knees, while Simon sat in the front with Tom.

They got to the Savoy about seven, the staff there not even raising an eyebrow at their evening clothes; presumably the mad idea of finishing off a party with breakfast there was commonplace to them. Cassie tried to avoid sitting next to Simon, but his hand went under her elbow and she was almost forced down into a chair. She glared at him, but he merely returned her look with one of cold menace. For the first time she felt the thrill of danger, but was so angry still that she could ignore it. It was a strange kind of anger, one that made her want to hit out at Simon and hurt. It wasn't only because he'd been late for his party, that was really the least part of it, it was also a fury that had grown out of her weeks of loneliness, of lack of love and sex, and in a crazy way it was also anger at herself for that brief flash of sexual awareness with Tom. She hadn't wanted it to happen, and it never would have if Simon hadn't insisted on taking the job in Scotland.

Strangely enough the meal was a happy one, not marred by marital friction at all, mainly because Julia and Chris were trying to outdo each other as the life and soul of the party, making jokes and puns that drew groans from the others. Poor John had given up all hope of his golf tournament and tried to join in, the bitchy remarks Julia had made earlier obviously having found a mark. Tom turned his attention to Sue, which helped to make up for the fact that her husband was virtually ignoring her, and she, too, began to enjoy herself.

From the moment that Simon had said he was coming with them he seemed to have taken over, organising the table, insisting they try the more exotic dishes and ordering champagne to drink, which made Julia tell him earnestly, but rather slurrily, that he was a man after her own heart. Cassie drank as much champagne as the others, but she didn't feel at all drunk or maudlin; she talked and laughed, clapped Chris when he did his party piece impression of Winston Churchill, but all the time felt as if her mind was amazingly clear and perceptive, her nerves taut and alert. She felt as if she had never had such control of her mind and emotions before.

It was gone nine before they left, Simon picking up the bill and refusing all offers to share. Julia was definitely tipsy when they came out and insisted that Chris help her along, putting her arm round him and whispering and giggling in his ear so that Cassie was afraid that she would give herself away and there would be a terrible scene, right there in the foyer of the Savoy. But Chris put his free arm round Sue and walked both women, his wife and his mistress, out to the car. Cassie, watching them with this new heightened perceptiveness, saw the sadistically triumphant look in his eyes and knew, suddenly, that he was enjoying himself. Enjoying having two attractive women loving him, wanting him, looking on him as the most important person in their lives. He had probably come to the party in the hope that something like this would happen, and was probably even getting pleasure out of making Sue miserable by neglecting her most of the evening, and by making Julia jealous when he did dance with his wife. He was behaving badly, had done so in coming to the party at all, but Cassie was more inclined to blame Julia; she had obviously given herself to him so wholeheartedly and humbly that he had begun to think he was God's gift to women and could do as he liked with them.

Cassie turned away, feeling suddenly revolted, and hurried to the car. She sat in the back as before, leaning back in the seat with her eyes closed, pretending a tiredness that was only physical, not mental. But the others, too, had grown weary and Sue was asleep on her husband's lap. Julia was awake, but quiet, and Cassie wondered if she, too, had seen that gleam of triumph in Chris's eyes.

The streets were busier now and Cassie was worried about John driving home.

'Stay here and get some rest for a few hours,' she urged him when they arrived back at the flat and he went to get in his car.

'No, no, I'm all right. I didn't have that much to drink, you know. And we've got to get back for the kids. Thanks for the party.' He bent to peck her cheek, then said awkwardly, 'Don't mean to interfere, Cass, but don't be too hard on old Simon, he would have made it if he could, you know.'

Cassie looked at him with a mixture of exasperation and pity. How men stuck together! Here was John trying to keep her from having a fight with Simon when his own marriage was disintegrating around his head and he didn't even know it!

They said goodbye to the others and waved them out of sight, then Cassie turned and walked quickly back up to the flat without even looking to see if Simon was following her. Once inside, she ignored the debris of the party and went straight into the bedroom to take off her jacket and throw it on a chair. Then she crossed to the bed, took her nightdress from under the pillow and made for the bathroom.

Simon came into the room, saw what she was doing and immediately barred her way.

'I want to talk to you,' he told her, his mouth set into a grim line.

'Well, I don't want to talk to you. I'm tired and I'm going to bed.'

'And you don't want to undress in front of me so you're going into the bathroom to change, is that it?'

'Yes, that's exactly it,' Cassie agreed, and went to move round him, but he swiftly stepped in front of her and grabbed her arms. 'Oh, no, you don't, we've got some talking to do first.'

'I've already told you that I've got nothing to say to you. Besides,' she added nastily, 'I wonder you've got the time to stop and talk. Surely you want to rush back to your beloved job.'

The grip on her arms tightened suddenly, but Simon merely said coldly, 'It isn't my job that's keeping us apart, Cassie, it's yours.'

She laughed jeeringly. 'Oh, that's right, put the blame on me! That's a typical male get out when they know they're in the wrong.'

Anger flamed in his eyes as he retorted, 'All right, so I didn't make the party and I'm sorry, but I tried, believe me I tried.'

'Oh, don't apologise to me,' Cassie parried, her voice as angry as his. 'Why don't you apologise to all the friends who took the trouble to come and bring you presents?' she said, remembering the pile of gaily-wrapped parcels that were waiting for him on a table in the sitting-room. 'After all,' she added bitterly, 'what the hell do I matter? I'm just the one who has to sit at home while you have a lovely time playing the power game in Scotland!'

Simon's jaw thrust forward angrily, and his eyes narrowed. 'All right, Cassie. You're obviously spoiling for a fight, so let's get it over.'

Furious words bubbled in her brain, words that would tell him of her loneliness and need, but in them lay only self-pity, so instead she went off at a tangent and bit out sarcastically, 'Oh, no, it isn't me who wants to fight. You were the one who . . .' she sought wildly for a descriptive enough word, 'who came *rampaging* in here and tried to knock Tom down. Is that the way you normally greet your old friends?'

A muscle jerked in his cheek and Simon's fingers bit into her arms, making her wince. 'That was sheer gut reaction. I walked in and saw you, apparently alone in the flat with another man. He had his arms round you and looked as if he'd been kissing you. How the hell did you expect me to react? And just what was he doing with his arms round you, anyway?'

Cassie's heart began to beat faster, she felt again an overwhelming urge to hurt him; a combination of anger, fatigue, too much drink, and nervous tension over a long period. Without giving herself time to think, she glared up at him and retorted, 'Maybe he was trying to comfort me in your absence.'

'What's that supposed to mean?' Simon demanded, a dangerous note in his voice now.

'Mean?' Cassie knew she had touched a raw spot and pushed the knife in. 'Why, nothing. But there again it could mean that I've been seeing a lot of Tom while you've been playing God in Scotland. It could mean that he had to take your place as host at the party so why the hell shouldn't he take your place in my bed?'

Immediately she'd said it, Cassie knew that she'd gone too far. Simon's eyes grew dark with murderous rage and she cried out with pain as his fingers dug into her flesh. For a moment she thought that he was going to lose control of himself and strike her. But then, his voice savage, he demanded through gritted teeth, 'Are you having an affair with him? Are you?' As he bit the questions out his emotion was so strong that he shook her, her whole body swaying with the force of it.

Cassie stared up at him, wanting to go on hurting but afraid now, afraid of the scarcely controlled fury in his face and the strength of his hands that gripped her so violently. If she pushed him too far and he lost that fragile control ... Turning her head away, she said, 'No. No, I'm not.'

Slowly the grip on her arms eased, relaxed. She looked up at Simon and saw that his eyes were still hard but they had lost their violence. She gave an inner sigh of relief, knowing that she was safe again, but her ungovernable temper made her add defiantly, 'Although it would serve you damn well right if I was. And anyway, I hardly expect that you've been leading a celibate life up there. You're no monk, Simon. I'm sure that you've found at least one girl to have sex with.'

'That isn't true and you know it!'

'No? I saw the way that hostess on the plane looked at you. It wouldn't surprise me if ...'

'Cassie, stop it!' His harsh voice ripped through her accusation as he moved his hands up to put them on either side of her face. 'Do you really believe what you're saying? Do you?'

His grey eyes stared down into hers, steady and unblinking. There was a white, set look to his mouth, the mouth that had kissed her and murmured endearments so many times. Anger gave way to pain and she closed her eyes, shutting out his face.

'No.'

'All right, then let's talk this through sensibly, shall we?' Slowly he drew his hands away and put them down at his sides, stood looking at her grimly. 'If you don't believe that I'm being unfaithful then why say it?' he demanded.

Cassie looked up at him mutely, her mouth set into an obstinate line. Her head ached and she felt deathly tired suddenly. Far too tired to try and put her feelings into words. Not that she even knew that she wanted to; somehow it just wasn't the time for words. Her head drooped and she shrugged her shoulders. 'I don't know. I don't know anything any more.' She pulled away from him and said heavily, 'I'm going to bed.'

For a moment it looked as if Simon was going to insist, but then he saw the dark shadows round her eyes and said, 'Maybe we could both do with some rest,' and moved out of the way so that she could go to the bathroom.

Usually Cassie took good care of her clothes, but that morning she just pulled them off and dropped them on the floor, uncaring. She creamed off her make-up and stood gazing unseeingly at her face in the mirror of the bathroom cabinet, wishing that the party last night had never happened, wishing that they could go back in time to before Simon had been offered the directorship. Not that it would have made any difference, she thought dully. If it hadn't been Scotland it would have been somewhere else. Sooner or later

Simon would have been offered promotion and he would have taken it, regardless of her wishes.

She put on her nightdress and went into the bedroom. The curtains were open and she pulled them closed, shutting out the mid-morning sunlight. It seemed strange to be going to bed in daylight. Simon came through the bedroom to the bathroom and she pulled the duvet up around her neck and turned on her side. She was so tired that she expected to fall asleep the moment her head touched the pillow, but her mind was still alert, defying her fatigue, and kept going back to the party, to Julia deceiving John with Chris and what the possible outcome would be. She wondered if Sue knew, whether she'd guessed last night. Restlessly Cassie turned over, trying to get more comfortable, trying to will herself to go to sleep. She tried counting, but had only got to seventeen when her thoughts wandered off as she remembered that electric moment with Tom. Would he have kissed her, kissed her properly? Almost from the beginning he had kissed her on the cheek in greeting and when saying good-night, but there was a world of difference in that sort of friendly peck and the look that had been in his eyes at that moment. And if he had tried to kiss her would she have let him? Cassie couldn't even pretend to herself that she would have been capable of any resistance. The sexual impact of the moment had been too great for that. And it had made her afraid. For the first time since she'd known Simon she had become attracted to another man, and it had happened at a time when she was vulnerable and alone. She desperately needed some kind of reassurance—wanted, really, to be taken in hand and have her life firmly put back in order again. And perhaps the way she had behaved towards Simon had been an instinctive urge to rouse his anger and make him do just that. She heard the door of the bathroom opening and immediately closed her eyes and pretended to be asleep.

Simon didn't come to bed straightaway, she could hear him moving about the room in the half light, going to the wardrobe and putting things inside, opening the drawers in the dresser and closing them again. All thoughts of sleep had fled now, she was too tense, too busy wondering what he would do. She heard him come over to the bed and tried to keep her breathing even as he pulled back the duvet and climbed gently into the bed beside her. He lay on his back, quite still. Their bodies weren't touching, but even so Cassie was tinglingly aware of his nearness, of his lean, strong body so close to her own. And it had been so long since they had made love—nearly three months. A white heat of desire tore through her and she yearned to turn to him, to make him hold her and love her, feel his skin against hers, feel the hardness of his body joining with hers and washing away all doubts, all fear, all frustration. The desire was so fierce that she almost moaned aloud, but bit her lip in time, pride and obstinacy refusing to allow her to be the one to make the first move.

But the steady rhythm of her breathing must have changed because Simon said shortly, 'There's really no point in pretending to be asleep, Cassie; I know you're awake.'

For a couple of seconds she toyed with going on with the pretence, but realised it was futile. 'Well, I am now,' she retorted in a hostile tone.

Putting out a hand, he pulled her over on to her back. His arm was bare.

'Why aren't you wearing pyjamas?' she demanded accusingly.

'Why do you always get prudish whenever we have a row?' Simon countered.

'I am *not* being prudish.'

'Then take this thing off.' Simon's tone had altered now, become soft, suggestive as he touched her nightdress.

'No. I told you I want to go to sleep.'

'Are you sure, Cassie? Are you really sure that's what you want?' His hand touched her neck, slid inside the opening of her nightdress and moved slowly down to caress her breast.

His touch roused her at once, sending a flame of sexuality coursing through her body. She wanted to say, yes, yes, that's what I want, but her stubborn pride wouldn't let her forgive him so easily, so quickly. Using all her will-power, she pulled away from him and snapped out, 'Take your hand off me! Just what right do you think you've got to walk in here after three whole months and expect to just have sex on demand?'

'What the hell have rights got to do with it?' Simon retorted exasperatedly. 'All right, so we've been apart for three months, isn't that all the more reason to make love now we're together?'

'Having sex isn't going to solve anything,' Cassie told him vehemently, so vehemently that she almost believed it. 'The same problems will still be there afterwards. It won't make any difference.'

Simon listened to her grimly, and then, his voice harsh, demanded, 'Since when did it become having sex instead of making love? What the hell's got into you, Cassie?' He propped himself up on one elbow and looked at her angrily.

'There's nothing the matter with me,' she returned hotly. 'I'm just pointing out that you can't come home and expect everything to be the way it was. I don't like being alone for months on end. Why, we might just as well not be married at all, for God's sake! And going to bed together isn't going to put things right, although men always think that it will, of course,' she added sardonically. 'They think that they've only got to exert a bit of masculinity and make a woman have sex and everything will be sweetness and light again. Well, it doesn't work!'

'Are you talking about men in general or me in particular?' Simon enquired, his voice cold.

'About all men, of course.'

'And I wonder just how you've suddenly come to know how men's minds work?' Simon remarked, his mouth set into a grim line. He wasn't touching her any more, not his hands nor any part of his long lean body. His grey eyes were ice-cold and there was a shut-in look about his face as if he had withdrawn into himself. 'But I'm afraid you won't be able to prove the truth of that statement, with me at any rate, because you've killed any desire I had for you stone dead. So go to sleep, Cassie, I won't disturb you.' His eyes glinted down at her, hard and enigmatic, then he added caustically, 'Sweet dreams, darling,' before rolling over with his back to her.

Cassie bit her lip and closed her eyes, trying to go to sleep, telling herself that she was glad she'd put him off. But her whole body ached with need, her hands balling into tight fists at her side to stop her from trembling. She risked a look at him in the dim light, but his back was still towards her, as hard and rigid as his uncompromising attitude. A rush of frustrated anger surged through her. Damn him! Damn him! Couldn't he see? Couldn't he understand that she wanted him to *make* her, to *force* her to do what he wanted? She wanted, needed, to fight him physically, to have him overpower her. Desperately she needed him to prove his mastery over her, so that she would once again know where and who she was. A primitive need, maybe, but her feelings now were raw and basic. She didn't want to make the first move towards a tentative reconciliation, she wanted to have it proved to her, without any shadow of a doubt, that Simon was the boss.

But he lay completely still, so still that she guessed he'd gone to sleep, and anger turned to a wave of pure hatred, so violent that it shocked her. She'd been angry with him many times before in the past, but never, never had she hated him. She lay still, gazing up at the ceiling, feeling bleak and miserable until at last she drifted into an exhausted sleep.

When she awoke, late in the afternoon, she yawned, still half asleep, and reached across the bed for Simon. But the bed was empty and she heard his muted voice in the sitting-room. Quickly she got up, showered and dressed, wondering who he had with him, but when she went into the room she found that he was talking on the telephone to someone who had been at the party, the pile of now unwrapped gifts on the low table in front of him. There was coffee, hot in the percolator. Cassie poured a large mug and carried it into the sitting-room, curled up on the settee and picked up the Sunday paper. Her head throbbed, but the coffee at least got rid of the dry, parched feeling in her mouth. She shouldn't have had any champagne with breakfast this morning; mixing her drinks always gave her a hangover. The thought of the Savoy made her remember her discovery of Julia's lover. Should she tell her she knew? Cassie wondered. But perhaps better not, better to keep out of it altogether.

Simon finished his conversation and looked across at her, but Cassie pretended to be engrossed in the paper, holding it up so that he couldn't see her face. After a moment he dialled again and spoke to another friend. He made two more calls, then put down the receiver decisively.

'I trust you slept well?' he enquired blandly.

'Yes, thank you.' Cassie turned a page, making sure that the paper still hid her from his view.

'Good. Thank you for the birthday presents, by the way.'

'I hope you like them,' Cassie returned stiltedly, remembering the care she'd taken on selecting the expensive sweater that she'd bought in Paris, and the cuff-links from the jewellery department in Marriott & Brown's.

'Very much. Are you feeling okay, quite rested?'

'I told you,' Cassie answered irritably, 'I'm perfectly well.'

'I'm glad.' He stood up, came over to her and jerked the paper out of her hands, dropping it on the floor. 'So now let's have that talk.' But as he sat down on the edge of the settee, he said deliberately, 'But first there's this.' And he leant forward and kissed her firmly on the mouth.

Taken by surprise, at first Cassie's lips were soft and yielding, but then they hardened as she quickly pulled away. For a brief second a bitter, fed-up look showed in Simon's eyes, but it was quickly masked as he said harshly, 'That was for the birthday present. And now you've got some explaining to do.' His eyes, cold as water over stone, bored into hers as he bit out, 'And we'll start by you telling me just how often you've been seeing Tom Rydell!'

Cassie stared at him, sensing his anger although he had it under control, and feeling glad that he was angry, willing to fuel it to enrage him further.

'What does it matter to you how often I go out with Tom? After all, you should be glad that one of your friends is willing to entertain me while you're up in Scotland playing . . .'

'Don't say that again, Cassie,' Simon put in savagely. 'Just don't say it!'

'All right. While you're up in Scotland *working*, then. Well, shouldn't you?' she demanded, when he didn't answer.

The corner of his mouth twisted scornfully. 'Be glad that some other man is taking my wife out? I don't think you know me very well, Cassie.'

'If you're not here to take me out, then why the hell shouldn't I go out with a friend?' she demanded, her voice rising.

Simon stood up and took an angry step away, turned, his hands shoved into his pockets. 'To go out with a friend from time to time is one thing, but you'd never even met Tom Rydell before he came to England. And don't try telling me that the friendship's platonic, because I won't believe it; no man and woman yet ever had a purely platonic relationship.' He reached forward suddenly and hauled her to her feet. 'And you still haven't told me how often you've been seeing him. How often, Cassie?' he demanded stridently.

His anger was out in the open now, she could feel it

in his hand that held her wrist like a vice, hear it in his voice, although he still had his features under control. And her own blood was running hot in her veins, pumping adrenalin into her heart so that it beat loud and fast, filling her with an intoxicating, bubbling kind of fear and excitement all mixed up together. From somewhere a small voice of sanity told her to play it cool, but it was lost beneath the fascination of seeing how far she could go, how far she could push him. Belligerently she replied, 'As often as possible.'

His face paled. 'And just how often is that?'

'Every weekend and almost every night during the week.'

His jaw tightened and his lips drew into a thin line. 'You said you weren't having an affair with him?'

'No, I'm not,' Cassie answered coolly, fiercely glad of the punishment she was inflicting.

'Has he asked you?'

'No.' His face relaxed a little so she added cruelly, 'But that doesn't mean that I won't say yes when he does.'

The hand holding hers jerked, and his fingers bit into her wrist and a flame of anger shot through his face. 'You bitch! You cold-hearted little bitch!' Hot, murderous rage shone in his eyes and Cassie, in a purely reflex action, lifted up her left arm as if to ward off a blow.

It never came. When she dared to look at Simon his face was still very white and there was a grim, bleak look in his grey eyes, but he had himself under control again. He let go of her wrist, pushed his hands in his pockets and moved away from her to stare out of the window. After a while he said curtly, 'I notice you said *when* he asked you and not if. Is it inevitable that he'll ask you, then?'

'I don't know.' Suddenly Cassie regretted what she'd done, felt ashamed. She put out a tentative hand to touch his sleeve. 'Simon, I . . .'

He pulled his arm free from her touch and moved away. The physical rejection hit her like a blow. He had no right to do that; she was the one who was supposed to be doing the rejecting!

Turning to face her, he said forcefully, 'I don't know why you're doing this, Cassie, but if going out with Tom is some kind of moral blackmail to make me jealous so that I'll give up my job, then it won't work. I don't like blackmail and even less do I like the people who perpetrate it. Nor do I go much on your using Tom as a tool.'

Colour flared in Cassie's cheeks. 'I'm not *using* him!'

'No? Then I feel sorry for him.' Simon paused, then went on heavily, 'I love you, Cassie. And I want us to be together. You felt that you couldn't live in Scotland and I could understand that and was willing to compromise. But now it seems that that doesn't satisfy you either; you want an all-out surrender to your wishes. But I'm not that kind of man, Cassie. And if you can't go on as we are, then it looks as if you're going to have to make a choice.'

'What—what choice?' Cassie's voice was little more than a whisper.

'Between me and your job.' He said it slowly, reluctantly, as if he found it hard to get the words out.

Cassie couldn't speak, could only stare at him numbly. She felt as if all the world had suddenly stopped and she was acutely aware of little things: of birds quarrelling outside the window, of the smell of stale tobacco that still hung in the room from the party, of the cold feeling that seemed to take her heart in its iron grip.

When she didn't speak Simon's voice hardened and he said roughly, 'And leave Tom out of this. He only complicates matters. It would be better if you didn't see him again.'

Without bothering to think of the consequences, Cassie let her ungovernable temper and constant need to assert her independence come to the fore and she answered defiantly, 'I shall see him whenever and as often as I like!'

Simon's lips drew back into a grim, sardonic smile. 'That's what I thought you'd say.' He turned on his heel and walked into the bedroom.

Cassie stared after him for a moment, cursing herself for a fool, then she followed him into the bedroom and saw that he was throwing some clothes into his overnight bag.

'Where are you going?' she asked.

'Back to Scotland.'

'Do you—have to go now?'

He gave that grim little smile again, a look that Cassie had never seen on his face before today and which she found frightened her to death.

'Why stay? There's nothing for me here.' He shut the case, shrugged himself into a jacket and walked past her as she stood in the doorway. At the door to the hall he paused and looked back. His voice polite, impersonal, as if he was speaking to his secretary or someone, he said, 'When you've made up your mind, perhaps you'll let me know.' He waited for a moment, but she could only stare at him dumbly, and so he gave a brief nod and walked out of the flat.

CHAPTER SEVEN

For a couple of days Cassie lived in a kind of vacuum, certain that Simon hadn't meant it, that he'd only issued his ultimatum in the heat of the moment and that he would soon ring and put everything right again. Only he didn't phone. The days lengthened into a week, but still he didn't call. Cassie rushed home every evening, firmly refusing all Tom's invitations for a date, just sitting alone and waiting for the phone to ring. When it did she would start up eagerly, her heart beating overtime, trying to compose her voice but still sounding husky and eager when she said the number. But always it was a friend, whom she would cut short in case Simon tried to call her and found the number engaged.

By the end of the week all certainty and self-confidence had gone. She drooped over her work and was short-tempered with her colleagues, who looked at her in surprise, knowing that she didn't suffer fools gladly but never having seen her in this sort of mood before. At the weekend she stayed at home, certain that Simon would phone then, even if it was only to find out if she was defying him, but the empty hours dragged on without interruption. All that did come to the flat that weekend was a letter from Tom saying how much he missed her company, that he would understand if Simon had forbidden her to see him, but that he very much wanted to go on with their friendship in any circumstances. With the letter came a huge bouquet of flowers, but it was the phrase 'if Simon has forbidden you to see me again', plus a growing anger and resentment, that finally made Cassie pick up the phone late on Sunday night and ring Tom. On the surface the call was to thank him for the flowers, but she only put up a half-hearted resistance when he tried to persuade her to see him again and she ended up by agreeing to have lunch with him the following day.

It was a gesture of defiance, really, but a rather pathetic, empty gesture when she couldn't throw it in Simon's face. And immediately she'd accepted she knew it was wrong. But it was only lunch, she told herself, having lunch with a man was quite acceptable. Everyone did it. In fact everyone seemed to be having affairs nowadays; only this week she'd heard that an old school friend was getting a divorce, of someone else who'd left home to live with a married man. It seemed that marriage was definitely 'out' this year. Sexual morals were like fashion, constantly changing, what outraged society one season was perfectly acceptable the next.

But it wasn't just lunch, of course. Having gained so much, Tom soon got her laughing again and persuaded her to have dinner the next day, and before she knew quite where she was, Cassie was gently coerced into seeing him almost as often as before. But always, as soon as she got home at night, the first thing she would do was to run the tape on the answer-phone hoping for a message from Simon. There were messages in plenty from other people, but from Simon there was nothing.

Worry and fear gave way to stubborn anger; if Simon thought he could wear her down so that she would give in, he was wrong. If he didn't love her enough to even phone her, then he could just go to hell!

Tom watched her as she went through all the range

of emotional feelings, from worried and unhappy, through angry and resentful, and waited until she was defiant again before showing his hand. He had been as attentive as usual during the month that had elapsed since the party, taking her out to meals and the theatre, making her laugh and forget for a blissful few hours the ultimatum hanging over her head. He had been careful not to make any kind of demands on her, until Cassie began to think that she had imagined that brief moment at the party when she thought that he had been going to kiss her. But one Friday night, when they had been out to a night-club for a meal and had danced until the small hours, he brought her home and, instead of giving her a light kiss goodnight and leaving her on her doorstep as he usually did, Tom purposefully strode into the flat, shut the door, took her in his arms and kissed her.

Cassie immediately tried to pull away, but his hand was at the back of her head, holding her still. Her mouth moved under his as she tried to protest, but he took advantage of it to force her lips apart, assaulting her mouth again and again as his kiss became deeper and passion took over.

Cassie's head swam, for a few moments longer she feebly tried to resist, but it had been so long since she'd been kissed, so long since she'd been loved. Her body ached with need, cried out to be touched, aroused. She gave a low moan and stopped fighting, surrendered her mouth to him. Tom made a small sound of triumph in his throat, his hand tightening in her hair as his mouth ravaged hers. At last he lifted his head, put a hand on either side of her face and gazed down at her, his breathing so unsteady that his body trembled, his eyes naked with desire.

'Cassie! Oh, honey.'

Slowly she opened her eyes, came back to reality. Panic filled her and she put up her arms to vainly try and push him away. 'No, Tom, please!'

But he wouldn't listen, holding her so that she couldn't escape and saying, 'Don't fight me, Cassie. You wanted me to kiss you as much as I did.'

'No, that isn't true.'

'Yes, it is. *Yes*. You've known how I felt about you ever since Simon's birthday party. But you've needed time to get over Simon, I've known that, and I've been willing to wait. But you're ready now, Cassie, ready to accept that he doesn't love you any more.'

Cassie stared at him in horror, appalled that he could make such sweeping assumptions, and even more that he obviously believed them. She gave an incredulous gasp, but before she could speak he was kissing her again, his lips demanding a response that she had no will-power to resist.

'Cassie darling,' he murmured against her hair, his voice thick and unsteady, 'I want to love you. Please let me love you.'

'Oh, Tom!' Her hands crept up round his neck as she looked into his face, then she leant her head on his shoulder and said, 'This is crazy. We both know it is.'

'Love is crazy. And, boy, am I crazy about you! Ever since the first moment I saw you I've wanted you.'

His voice went on above her head, saying the kind of things that every woman loves to hear, even though they were from the wrong man. Cassie could hear his heart beating loud beneath her head, his hands gently stroking her shoulders, his lips touching her hair. Closing her eyes, she lost herself in the pure sensuality of his embrace, let him go on doing what he wanted, caressing her with his voice, his hands. But then his hand moved down to her breast, like five fingers of fire that burned through her skin. She gave a gasp of pleasure, then jerked quickly out of his embrace.

She stood a good yard away, staring at him, her body trembling and her breathing scared, uneven. 'I want you to go. Please, Tom.'

He grinned, sure of himself, and moved towards her. 'No, you don't. You . . .'

'If you touch me again I'll scream!' Cassie's voice rose and there was an hysterical edge to it that made him stop precipitately.

Frowning, he said, 'What is this, honey? Don't say you didn't want me to kiss you.'

'No—I don't know.' Cassie shook her head in confusion and brought her hands up in front of her defensively. 'Please, Tom, just go!'

'Go? After this?'

'Yes.'

He looked at her for a long moment, then shrugged. 'Okay, if that's what you want.'

Moving towards the front door, he put out a hand to open it, but turned towards her again before he did so. 'Aren't you going to say goodnight?'

'Goodnight, Tom.'

'No, like this.' Before she was even aware of what he was going to do, he had taken a swift stride towards her, caught hold of her arm and backed her against the wall. Then he bent his head and kissed her for the third time. He put everything he had into that kiss, and he was very experienced, had been around. Cassie was lost after the first few seconds and emerged with her head in a whirl, her body quivering with awareness.

'Don't send me away, Cassie. Let me stay. I want you so much, so very much.' His voice was in her ear, soft and persuasive as his lips caressed her neck, her throat, the curve of her chin.

Her desire to be loved almost overwhelmed her. It would be so easy to yield, to say yes. And what difference would it make, no one would ever know. Simon didn't love her, he'd left her alone. It would serve him right if she gave herself to another man. She'd warned him that she would, hadn't she, and he'd still gone away. Demon reasons rose up to tempt her to say yes, and it would be so nice, so easy. His lips were hot against her skin, his hands firm as they caressed her quivering body.

But then tears spilled out of her eyes and she began to cry, the sobs catching in her throat. Startled, Tom raised his head, consternation in his blue eyes.

'Cassie, don't. Honey, please don't cry.' He tried to stroke her shoulders soothingly, but Cassie had her hands up to her face and was crying without restraint. 'Here.' He thrust a large handkerchief into her hand and then took her by the arm and led her back into the sitting-room and helped her sit down on the settee.

He moved away, but Cassie hardly noticed. Her whole body was racked by sobs as all the pent-up tensions and emotions of the last month broke through at last.

'Cassie, honey. C'mon, I want you to drink this.' Tom was kneeling on the floor beside the settee, a glass of amber-coloured brandy in his hand.

At first she shook her head in refusal, but he insisted and it was easier to obey than fight, so she gulped it down, the spirit making her cough, but easing the heartbreaking sobs so that she sat passively, her body quivering as the silent tears ran down her cheeks.

Tom sat down beside her and took her in his arms, resting her head on his shoulder. He stroked her hair gently until she'd cried herself out.

'I'm—I'm sorry.' Her voice was muffled against his chest.

'No, I'm the one that's sorry. I didn't realise—how much Simon meant to you.'

'What do you mean?' Cassie tilted her head to look at him.

'I thought you two were more or less through before I came along. That Simon had gone to live in Scotland because you weren't happy together.'

'No, it was because neither of us wanted to give up our jobs.'

Tom frowned. 'Are you saying, then, that you've never been unfaithful to Simon? That I'm the first man who's asked you?'

Cassie sat up straight and wiped her face with his handkerchief. 'If you don't mind, I'd like you to go now. I'm very tired.'

'Sure.' He stood up and looked down at her where she sat on the settee, head bent, not looking at him. 'Are you sure you'll be okay alone?'

'Quite sure, thank you.' But there was a break in her voice that she couldn't disguise as another tremor of emotion ran through her body.

'I'll call you tomorrow.'

'No, don't bother. I'll be all right. Really.'

He reached down and gently touched her hair. 'You know, Cassie, when I first met you I thought that you were a typical career girl, tough and self-sufficient, not really needing a man except as an escort and for sex. Then I realised you weren't the type who would have a casual affair, so I played it cool, but I still thought you were strong and independent enough to shrug off a marriage that hadn't worked out.' He paused, then added wonderingly, 'But now I see that I've been wrong about you all along. Underneath that self-confident act you put on you're as soft and fragile as delicate china. I'd no idea just how badly Simon had hurt you.' The pressure of his hand increased for a moment; he said, 'Goodnight, Cassie,' rather abruptly and then turned and let himself out of the flat.

He came back the following afternoon, ringing the doorbell continuously when she didn't open the door after his first ring. Cassie had slept late after not being able to get to sleep for hours the night before. She had bathed and put on a housecoat, but her face was unmade-up, her hair lying loose on her shoulders. She didn't say anything when she saw who it was, just turned and walked ahead of him into the kitchen.

'I'm making coffee, would you like a cup?' she asked without looking round.

'That would be fine.' Tom leaned against the door jamb; it was raining outside and he had on one of those trench-coat type macs that Americans always seemed to wear. He was watching her closely, broodingly almost.

As she put out another mug, Cassie said stiltedly, 'I'm sorry you were on the receiving end of my crying jag last night.'

Unexpectedly, Tom answered, 'I'm *glad* I was. It helped me to see things a whole lot clearer.' He stepped forward and put his hands on her shoulders, gently but insistently turning her round to face him. Then he kissed her, softly and very tenderly. 'You look so young today, so vulnerable,' he murmured as he lifted his head.

Cassie bit her lip, started to say determinedly, 'Look, Tom, I . . .' but just then the kettle boiled and she had to stop and turn it off.

She carried their coffee mugs into the sitting-room while Tom took off his coat, and she took care to sit in an armchair instead of the settee. Tom sat down and watched her, making no attempt to drink his coffee.

Cassie lowered her head, unable to meet his eyes. 'Don't—look at me like that.'

'Like what?'

'As if—oh, you know perfectly well what I mean.'

'As if I think you're wonderful, d'you mean?'

Cassie's eyes flew to meet his, then as quickly away again. 'N-no, that isn't what I meant,' she answered unsteadily.

'But it's true.' He stood up and took the mug from her nerveless fingers, set it on the table so that the steam rose and disappeared into the air. Then he pulled her to her feet and held her arms as he gazed down into her face. 'Don't look so scared.' He bent to kiss her but she turned her head away.

'Tom, I don't want this. Please stop.'

'I can't. You see,' he added, 'I've fallen in love with you.'

Cassie turned to stare at him unbelievingly. 'But—but you can't have!'

He gave a lopsided grin. 'No two ways about it, honey. I've fallen for you hard. I started off by just wanting you, but now I love you—very much.'

'No!' She tried to pull away, but he wouldn't let her.

'Yes, Cassie. I love you and I want very much to go to bed with you—to show you just how much I love you. I need you, honey. And last night proved that you need me.'

'No,' she repeated, and this time succeeded in pulling herself free. 'Do you know what you're saying?' she demanded agitatedly. 'You're asking me to be unfaithful to Simon!'

'Yes, I suppose I am.'

But he didn't seem particularly disturbed, so Cassie added forcefully, 'You're asking me to—to commit adultery!' The word sounded all the more shocking for being said out loud, and they were both a little stunned by it.

'That's an antiquated way of describing it. Can't you just admit that marrying Simon was a big mistake?'

'I thought he was supposed to be a friend of yours?' she said accusingly.

He shrugged. 'All's fair in love and war, Cassie.'

She began to feel angry and her lip curled scornfully. 'What a useful little saying that is! People always trot it out when they want an excuse for doing something wrong or underhand.'

Tom's tone hardened. 'Is it underhand to fall in love? Is it wrong to want the fulfilment of that love?'

Her face paled and she answered in little more than a whisper. 'No. No, it isn't.'

'And I love you, Cassie. So help me God, I do.'

He made a move towards her, but she moved away, her eyes wide and troubled in her pale face.

'It's—it's no use, Tom. I'm sorry, but I can't.' She held up a hand to stop him as he began to speak. 'I know what you're going to say: that if I didn't care for you I wouldn't have responded like I did last night. And it's true, I do care for you.' She looked down at her hands, gripping them together. 'I like you a lot. You've—you've made these last few weeks bearable for me, and I'm very grateful.' She hesitated a moment, then lifted her head and looked at him steadily. 'But I'm not going to go to bed with you, Tom. I'm just not the type. I couldn't live with myself afterwards, and I most certainly couldn't go on living with Simon, not live with him and pretend that nothing had happened. And anyway, it wouldn't be fair to anyone. Not to Simon, to me, or most of all you.'

'Just how do you work that out?'

'Because you'd never know whether I was doing it because I wanted to, or just because I was lonely and needed someone, or even,' she bit her lip, 'or even just to punish Simon. I wouldn't even know why myself,' she added slowly.

There was a long pause before Tom said hollowly, 'Yeah, I see what you mean.' He came to her and took hold of her hands, that were still agitatedly entwined, held them firmly in his own. 'Okay, so we'll get married.'

Cassie stared at him bug-eyed and opened her mouth to protest, but Tom put his hand over it.

'Don't say anything yet, just think about it. Divorce is easy nowadays and you wouldn't have to do a thing; I'll get my lawyers to arrange it. We could be married within months.'

Slowly he took his hand away as she continued to stare at him. 'But I—but I don't know that I *want* to marry you.'

He grinned suddenly. 'Do you know that you don't?'

She shook her head, putting her fingers up tiredly to her temples. 'I don't know anything any more.'

Tom left soon after, left her to sit alone wondering what to do. At times she was angry with Tom for having forced her into this, at other times glad because she knew she had to do *something*, she couldn't have gone on for much longer as she was. But most of all she hated Simon for ruining her life, for taking away her happiness and security, for even giving another man a chance to come into her life. At eleven o'clock, when it was perfectly obvious, even to the wildest hope, that Simon wasn't going to phone yet again, Cassie picked up a large vase that had been a wedding present from one of his relations, and hurled it against the wall with all her strength, shattering it into a dozen pieces.

She refused to give Tom an immediate answer, even though he pressed her to. She said that she wanted time to think it over, but perhaps she was subconsciously still hoping that Simon would phone or come home, but conscious hope was nearly dead.

About that time a new problem arose at work: Mrs Nichols, the buyer who had been put in temporary charge of the whole fashion department, put her foot down and refused to allow Cassie to make any more changes in her departments until they'd seen the results of the ones she had already made. They had an argument about it and Cassie went over her head to Mr Jepps, the head buyer, and to her surprise and resentment he backed up Mrs Nichols. Oh, he was nice about it, and sympathetic up to a point, but insisted that Mrs Nichols was in charge and that Cassie had to be governed by her decisions.

Going back to her office, Cassie threw herself down into her chair, thoroughly fed up, all her bright dreams for the new departments disappearing into a haze of red tape and petty officialdom. Moodily she looked at her desk where she had been designing a new carousel-type layout for the separates department that would display every colour range for the sweaters and cardigans. Picking up a thick, felt-tipped pen, she viciously drew two great lines across the drawing.

Sue happened to walk into the office at that moment and stared in consternation. 'What on earth . . .?'

Cassie stood up decisively and picked up her bag. 'Come on, Sue, we're going out to lunch.'

'But it's not even twelve o'clock!'

'So what? We're going anyway.'

Instead of going to the staff restaurant, Cassie marched out of the store and down a side street to a pub. She bought them each a drink and then told Sue what had happened. They discussed it at some length, but they both knew that there was nothing they could do.

'It's just bureaucracy gone mad,' Cassie complained. 'Just because Mrs Nichols has been there since the year dot they have to put her in charge. But her ideas are way out of date, Sue, they really are.'

She lit another cigarette straight after the last and drew on it gloomily.

'You're smoking too much,' Sue told her.

'I know.' Cassie looked at the cigarette distastefully and ground it out. 'I don't even like the things.' She glanced at Sue. 'You're smoking too,' she pointed out. Sue didn't say anything and after a moment Cassie asked rather uncertainly, 'How's Chris? Is he still doing that extra work?'

The younger girl didn't answer straightaway, sat looking at the smoke rising from her cigarette, then, her voice over-bright, she said, 'Oh, he's fine. He's still working late a lot, only . . .' her voice broke, 'only I don't think he's working at all, I think he's found another woman!' And tears spilled down her cheeks.

'Oh, God!' Hastily Cassie pulled a hanky out of her bag and thrust it into Sue's hands. 'Come on, let's get out of here.'

She led Sue into a nearby park where they found an empty bench, and there Sue poured it all out; her growing suspicions, the tell-tale hairs on his jacket and smudges of lipstick on his shirt. 'And then—and then,' poor Sue sobbed on, 'I walked into the bathroom one night while he was showering and he had scratches down his back and—and a bite mark on his shoulder.'

'Did you—say anything to him?'

Sue shook her head. 'No, I couldn't.' She looked at Cassie. 'Why do you think he did it? I know I'm not very experienced because there wasn't anyone before Chris, but I'm not frigid, or anything. And we've been married such a short time.'

'I don't know.' Cassie shook her head grimly. 'I'm the last person you should ask. What are you going to do?'

Sue sighed. 'I don't know. But I'm not going to let him go on deceiving me,' she added with sudden strength. 'I'm going to tell him that I know. Then he can either give this woman up, whoever she is, or leave.'

'And if he chooses to stay,' Cassie asked, 'will you be able to forgive him?'

Her eyes dark and troubled, Sue thought for a moment, then answered slowly, 'Yes, I think I'll be able to forgive him because I love him and need him, but I don't think I'll ever be able to forget what he's done.'

Cassie could think of nothing else but her conversation with Sue all day, it pushed everything else to the back of her mind. The poor girl had been so unhappy, her whole life shattered. Oh, God, why did men have to be such swine? She sat at home brooding about it for a long time, staring at the phone as she'd sat and stared for so many nights, then she slowly picked up the receiver and dialled Simon's number.

For a few minutes, when he answered, she couldn't speak. It had been so long since she'd heard his voice, such a long time.

'Who is that?' Simon demanded, then, his tone altering, 'Cassie? Is that you?'

'Yes.' Somehow she got the word out, though her voice was ragged.

'How are you?'

'I'm—I'm fine. You?'

'I'm very well.' There was a pause in which Cassie's throat was so tight she couldn't speak or even think of anything to say, broken when Simon said, 'Did you want me for anything special?'

Cassie's heart cried out, oh yes, for something very special, my darling. I want you to come home, to take care of me and love me again. But just as she opened her mouth to pour it all out, she heard another voice, a woman's voice on the other end of the line. The woman started to speak and then stopped abruptly.

Simon said urgently, 'Cassie? Look, I . . .'

She interrupted immediately, her tone cold and impersonal. 'No, not really. I've had a letter from the tennis club wanting to know if you're going to renew your subscription. And there are letters from your insurance company and your old college about a reunion dinner. Do you want me to deal with them or shall I send them on to you?'

'Perhaps I'll be able to deal with them myself. I might be able to get down to London next weekend.'

'Come by all means,' Cassie agreed briskly. 'I'll leave
the letters in the desk for you. I shan't be here myself—
I'm going on a buying trip to Italy. Goodbye, Simon,'
she added, putting the receiver down before he could
say anything else.

A thousand times during the following week Cassie
cursed herself for a fool for having made that phone
call. It had been a cry for help that had rebounded to
slap her in the face. Now she was tortured by pictures
of Simon with another woman, and the idea made her
feel physically sick. But it was just another misery to
add to the generally wretched tide in her life. Nothing
seemed to go right at work; goods didn't arrive or were
found to be below standard and had to be sent back,
Sue was upset most of the time, which made Cassie,
knowing that Chris and Julia had met at her house,
feel responsible. She couldn't sleep at night, lying
awake for hours on end and feeling like death when
she dragged herself to work in the morning. Tom, too,
was pushing her to make a decision because he would
have to go back to the States soon. Added to which the
weather was continuously wet and cloudy, typical
London weather when it seemed that summer would
never come. All in all, Cassie just wanted to stop the
world and get off, feeling that if she had to cope with
anything else she'd end up having a nervous break-
down.

As the week went on she felt so beset on all sides
that she knew she just had to get away and be alone.
There was no way she could go to Milan and buy
clothes for the store; she would probably order all the
wrong things and give Mrs Nichols a weapon to hold
against her. So she offered the trip to Sue, who jumped
at it, eager to get away from her own problems for a

few days. Cassie had already told Tom that she was going to Italy and was on the point of phoning him to tell him of her altered plans when she changed her mind. Perhaps it would do her good to be by herself for a while, to get right away from the flat and all its memories and go somewhere where she could think things through without any outside influences.

So early on the Saturday morning, Cassie packed a holdall with a few essentials and took a train out of London towards the south coast. There were a lot of people on the train heading for the seaside, but she got off at Taunton and caught a bus headed inland into Somerset, which took her on an unhurried, meandering route through sleepy villages of stone and thatch cottages until it pulled up outside a small hotel that looked as if it was still in the last century, where Cassie got off and booked a room.

The plumbing, too, seemed pretty ancient, but Cassie didn't care. She spent the whole two days walking round the countryside or sitting on a wall gazing at the view, and, in the evening, lying on her bed, watching the moon through the little dormer window set under the eaves. It rained most of the time, but that didn't matter either, in fact it seemed to wash away many of her doubts and uncertainties, leaving only the bare essentials, so that for the first time in many weeks she saw her way clear before her.

At first she had been filled with anger about Simon and the woman he'd been with, but then she tried to put herself in his place and realised that he must be feeling exactly the same way about her and Tom, and perhaps with more cause. She had turned to Tom out of loneliness, and might not Simon, too, be feeling just as lonely, as much in need of love and companionship, the things which she had bluntly refused to give him? And Tom? Did she love him enough to divorce Simon and marry him? She tried to foresee a future with him and couldn't, it just wasn't there! The only future she could ever envisage was with Simon, and God help her, she had been on the point of throwing it away. But perhaps it wasn't too late; their love for each other had been very strong, perhaps it was still strong enough to overcome what had happened.

On Sunday evening Cassie began the journey back to London, phoning Tom before she caught the train at Taunton and asking him to meet her at the station. He was waiting for her at the end of the platform, casually dressed in jeans and sweater and looking so masculine and virile that he drew every female eye in the place. Cassie knew now that she didn't love him, but as she walked towards him she realised the power of his attraction and how, for a while, it had gone to her head to be loved and wanted by such a man. But what girl's head wouldn't be turned by him? He was everything a woman could want—but he wasn't Simon.

And that was, more or less, what she told him as he drove her home through the wet streets.

He didn't take her refusal without a fight, at first trying argument and persuasion to make her change her mind and then abruptly stopping the car and taking her in his arms to try and persuade her that way, but she held out against it all, her determination strong enough to withstand all his arguments. At last Tom had to accept it and started the car again to drive her home. He pulled up outside the block of flats and sat looking bleakly out of the windscreen, his hands tight on the wheel.

'I guess this is goodbye, then?'

'Yes. I'm sorry, Tom. What will you do?' she asked tentatively. 'Go back to America?'

'I guess so.' He turned his head to look at her. 'What if Simon doesn't want you?'

Cassie winced at his bluntness but answered steadily. 'It doesn't make any difference. I'll just—live by myself.'

'He'll take you back, he'd be a damn fool not to.' Tom's hand came out to cover hers for a moment, then he abruptly got out of the car and came round to open her door for her. 'Goodbye, Cassie.'

She looked at him uncertainly. 'Goodbye, Tom.'

He shut the car door and looked as if he was going to walk away, but then he turned back and lunged for her, pulling her into his arms and kissing her with a compulsive passion. 'Cassie! Oh, God. If you ever need me . . . just remember I love you!' He kissed her again, then let her go so suddenly that she almost fell. The next moment he was in the car and pulling away fast out into the road.

Cassie watched him out of sight, then turned and slowly climbed the stairs to the flat. It was late, she'd been with Tom a long time, and she felt tired, but pleasantly so. Now maybe she could start building her life again.

The light was on in the hall and she blinked in surprise, then hurried into the sitting-room. Simon was there. He was standing at the uncurtained window that overlooked the entrance to the block of flats.

'Simon!' Cassie's face lit up when she saw him and she started towards him, then stopped as he turned and she saw the cold, harsh look on his face. 'Simon?'

she said again, her heart filled with uncertainty and foreboding.

'Did you have a good trip?' His voice, too, was cold as the wind in winter.

'Why—why, yes, I suppose so.'

His eyes ran over her, taking in her casual clothes and the holdall. 'Was that all the luggage you took with you?'

Cassie frowned, trying to work out why he was like this, what he was getting at. 'Yes, I didn't need very much.'

A look of such savage fury came into his face that it frightened her. 'No, I don't suppose you do need much when you're spending the whole weekend in bed with your lover!'

She stared at him, appalled as much by his assumption as his fury. 'No, I didn't. I . . .'

'You bitch! Don't lie to me. I *saw* you out there with him!' He pointed savagely at the window. 'Do you understand? I saw you!'

'It's you who doesn't understand,' Cassie put in desperately, but Simon hardly heard her.

'I thought if I gave you enough time you'd come to your senses,' he swept on furiously. 'I thought that when you phoned me it was a way of saying that you were ready for us to talk things out, but now I see that it was just to lie to me about going to Italy, to make sure I wouldn't come down this weekend.' His mouth pulled back into a sneer. 'But why bother to lie, Cassie? And why bother to go away for the weekend? Surely, if you're going to behave like a cheap little slut, you're not too fastidious to do it here in our marriage bed!'

Cassie stared at him, too shaken for a moment to speak, then anger ripped through her like a flame. She went for him with her fists and feet, hitting out at his face and trying to kick him. Simon swore savagely as one or two punches landed, then caught hold of her wrists, twisting them cruelly, then with disdainful ease propelled her backwards and shoved her forcefully down on to the settee. He looked down on her for a moment as she lay winded, his face contorted by rage and disgust, then he wiped his hands as if he'd just touched something dirty, picked up his case and left her lying there.

Staggering to her feet, Cassie called his name and went to run after him, but the coffee table had been knocked over in their fight and she tripped over it, cutting her hand on some broken glass. By the time she got down to the entrance of the block of flats it was too late, he was gone.

The following night she again dialled Simon's number. When he answered it she said, coldly and without preamble, 'I want a divorce.'

CHAPTER EIGHT

THERE was a long pause on the line, then Simon replied, 'Very well. I can't get down to London again for a while, you'll have to come up here and discuss it.'

'I don't see why we have to discuss it at all,' Cassie answered baldly. 'Why can't we just let our solicitors handle it?'

'Divorce can be an expensive business; why pay lawyers when we could probably save time and money by working out how we're going to set about it first?'

'I don't care how much it costs. I just want to be free of you.'

There was an almost tangible silence before Simon said coldly, 'As Tom Rydell's obviously paying your expenses I don't expect you do care about cost, but presumably you do care about the time factor, in which case you'll have to come up here.'

'No.'

'If you want a divorce you'll have to. And come alone, this is between you and me. I don't want Rydell here.'

Cassie recognised that tone of voice and knew there was no arguing with it. After a few minutes she said, 'All right, I'll come up on Saturday.'

'I'll make arrangements with Mullaine's to fly you in the firm's plane.'

'I'll make my own way up, thanks,' Cassie put in sardonically.

'Suit yourself. But you'll have to take their helicopter

out here from Glasgow. There's one leaving at three in the afternoon.'

'All right.'

Cassie snapped the receiver down, her hand trembling, not trusting herself to talk any longer without breaking down.

On Saturday morning she dressed with extra care, putting on a tight-skirted blue woollen suit and a cream silk blouse with ruffles and a bow at the neck. Her make-up and hair she made sure were as perfect as she could get them, because she was going to need all the confidence that looking good could give her when she met Simon. The journey up in the train was long and uneventful, giving her plenty of time to think about what she would say to him. All hope of a reconciliation had gone now, driven out by the unjust assumptions he'd made about her and Tom and the things he'd called her. What hope could there possibly be after that?

She was too uptight and nervous to be able to eat when she reached Glasgow, so she hired a cab and went straight to the airport, sitting in the waiting-room with her hands clasped tightly together in her lap until it was time to get in the helicopter. Surprisingly, it wasn't raining as she was led across the tarmac, but the skies were grey and cloudy and there was no warmth in the air. The day felt as cold and miserable as her heart.

There were very few passengers today, only another woman a few years older than herself who had a tiny baby in her arms and was being pushed towards the helicopter in a wheelchair, obviously fresh out of a maternity hospital, and a man in a business suit carrying a bulging briefcase. They were led to a much smaller helicopter than the one Cassie had travelled

in before; this one held only four passengers besides
the pilot. They climbed aboard, the new mother being
carefully helped out of the wheelchair and into her seat,
the safety-belt being put round her and the baby. Then
Cassie got in, followed by the male passenger. The
other woman smiled at her as Cassie fastened her own
belt and looked as if she wanted to talk, but Cassie
gave only a perfunctory smile in return; she was too
tense and strung up to be able to make small talk now.
But luckily the noise of the engine and the rotor blades
was so loud that talk was impossible anyway and she
was able to sit back thankfully in her seat and lose
herself in her own thoughts as the helicopter rose into
the air and began the long flight up the coast to
Kinray.

It must have been at least half an hour later when
Cassie realised there was something wrong. She had
been so wrapped up in her own problems that she had
been taking no notice at all of what was going on
around her, and it was only when the man next to her
knocked her arm as he sat forward, his body tense,
that she came back to reality. She looked round, wondering at first what was the matter, then saw that they
were flying in a thick, swirling mist that enclosed them
like a cloud. Cassie peered out of the window, but there
was no sign of the ground, the mist was all around
them. The pilot had the windscreen wipers going and
was talking on the radio, his voice, although she
couldn't distinguish the words, sounding urgent. On
her other side the woman's eyes were wide and scared
and she was holding her baby tightly.

'What is it?' Cassie raised her voice above the noise
of the engine.

The man next to her shouted back, 'The mist came

down suddenly and he can't see. And there's high ground ahead.'

'But—but surely he's got instruments and things . . .' Her voice died in her throat as she realised just how little she knew about helicopters; they were just another of the machines—like cars and planes—that you always took for granted until something went wrong with them. And this time it looked as if there was something seriously wrong.

By straining her ears she could make out the pilot calling over the radio, but he didn't seem to be getting any reply because he kept repeating the same things. They seemed to be going more slowly now, but it was impossible to guess at what height they were flying when she couldn't see the ground.

The pilot turned round and gestured downwards with his thumb, shouting, 'Hold on—I'm going down. It might be clear there.'

The helicopter swayed to the right and then began to swoop downwards. Cassie felt fear grip her heart and she clutched the arms of her seat, gripping them till the knuckles showed white. Beside her the woman gave a sob of fright, then clutched wildly at Cassie's sleeve. 'My baby! Help me hold him.'

Cassie stared at her, and it took all the courage she had to let go of the seat arm, turn towards the woman and put her arm across to help her hold the baby, which was crying now, either from being held too tightly or because it had sensed its mother's fear.

Things began to happen so quickly then that they merged into a jumbled kaleidoscope of terror when there was no time to think, only to react to the primitive urge for self-preservation. Cassie remembered the mist clearing for a brief second and seeing the sea below them, but close, only a few yards away. Someone shouted and the helicopter rose again, but then it banked sharply, throwing her violently back in her seat. The woman began to scream shrilly, but Cassie could only stare in appalled horror as she saw a wall of rock appear in front of them, rising out of sight above them. The pilot did something to the controls that made the aircraft turn violently to the right, throwing them about so that the man beside her was jerked almost out of his seat and was half lying on her. Cassie's stomach came up into her throat and for a few seconds she could hardly breathe, felt as if she was going to suffocate. She put up feeble hands to try and push the man off, but suddenly they were the right way up again and the helicopter was going down. It met the ground with a terrific bump, then tilted over to one side. Cassie was sure that they'd come down in the sea and expected every second to see water come pouring in to drown them where they sat.

But the pilot was taking off his safety strap and pushing the door open, yelling at them to get out. Somehow Cassie managed to make her fingers work, to pull at the strap until it came free, but the woman next to her was screaming hysterically, making no move to undo her strap, just holding the baby and screaming, her eyes starting from her head. The pilot got out of his seat, pushed past Cassie and hit the other woman sharply across the face; the screaming stopped as if someone had turned off a radio. The other passenger had got his door open and was jumping out. Cassie scrambled out of her seat and moved to follow him.

'Keep your heads down!' the pilot yelled across at her. 'The rotors are still going round.'

It looked an awfully long way down, but the man had turned and was holding out a hand to her. Cassie took it and jumped, landing in water and soft sand. She saw that they had landed on the tiny beach of a small sea-locked bay with tall rugged cliffs all around it. The sound of the sea breaking on the rocky shore was very loud, that and the gradually slowing rotor blades.

'You'll have to help me,' the pilot shouted to them. 'I can't get her out.'

They waded round the front of the helicopter and Cassie saw with horror that it was balanced precariously with one rail on the edge of a large rock, in danger of slipping sideways at any moment. The woman had frozen with fear, clutching the baby to her breast and refusing to move.

'Come on, you've got to get out. It could go over at any moment!' The pilot had undone her strap and was trying to pull the woman out, but she wouldn't come. In desperation he snatched the baby out of her arms and gave it to Cassie. 'Get going. Run!' he yelled at her.

As Cassie turned to obey him she saw the woman scream like a wounded animal and almost fall out of the helicopter into the pilot's arms, her fear for her baby greater than her own. The two men picked the woman up between them and began to run through the shallows towards the beach as fast as they could. Cassie's high-heeled shoes sank into the sand at every stop and she impatiently kicked them off. The shingle cut into her feet, but at least she could run.

Behind her she heard a noise and turned to see the helicopter start to slip off the rock, the rotor blades, which were still spinning round, only much slower now, gradually getting nearer the ground.

'Get down!'

Even as the pilot yelled a warning Cassie saw the danger and dropped to the ground, somehow managing to hold the baby out of the water. There was an almighty snapping sound as the first rotor hit the ground. Churned-up shingle flew with the velocity of bullets, all mixed up with sea spray and chunks of broken metal that whistled overhead and smashed against the stone cliffs, some of them ricocheting off to make a double danger. The second rotor blade hit and then the third, turning the beach into a nightmare of flying missiles and debris. Cassie heard a cry of pain behind her and was almost soaked by the spray of water, but then there was only the sound of the waves, breaking everlastingly over the shore.

Slowly she picked herself up and looked around. The baby was crying lustily, so that was all right. The two men had covered the woman with their own bodies, but the male passenger had blood coming from a wound in his back. Somehow they managed to wade on to the beach, the pilot more or less carrying the baby's mother. He set the woman down on the sand, leaning against the cliff face, and Cassie gave her her baby, then they helped the injured man off with his jacket so that the pilot could look at the wound.

'Do you know anything about nursing?' the pilot asked her.

Cassie shook her head. 'I'm afraid not.'

'There's a first aid box in the chopper; I'll go back and see if I can get it.'

He waded out to the now half-submerged helicopter and Cassie looked at the other man worriedly. 'Does it hurt very much?'

He shook his head. 'I'm so bloody wet I can't feel it. My name's Bill, by the way—Bill Harris.'

'Mine's Cassie Ventris.' He seemed to be all right, so Cassie turned towards the young mother and repeated her name, adding, 'How are you feeling?'

'Not too bad. And the baby's all right, that's the main thing,' the woman answered with a pleasant Scots accent.

'Yes, of course. Is he your first baby?'

'Yes.' The woman looked up at Cassie. 'We've waited so long for him—nearly nine years. I lost three others—I kept having miscarriages. I had to stay in bed for over five months to make sure I kept him. And now this—now this has to happen!' The woman burst into tears and began to cry noisily.

'Oh, don't. Please hush. We're safe now. Look, what's your name?'

'Jeannie—Jeannie Cooper. I'm sorry, I'm a bit low at the moment.'

'Of course you are.' Cassie stayed and talked to her while the pilot put a dressing on Bill Harris's back. They were all wet through, but there was no wind to chill them, and Cassie could only be glad that it was summertime; if it had happened in the winter they wouldn't have stood a chance.

When the pilot had finished he looked about him and then up at the cliffs. 'I'd better try and climb those and see if I can get help.'

'Didn't you manage to send off a radio message?' Bill Harris asked.

'I tried, but the cliffs must have been bouncing the signal back; there was a lot of interference and I was having trouble with the radio before we ditched.'

'Could a helicopter pick us up from here?'

'No.' The pilot shook his head. 'The cliffs are too close. The only thing I can do is go up. I've brought some flares from the chopper; I'll take a couple of them with me and if I hear or see anything I'll send one up.'

He walked round the little bay until he found a broken patch of cliff and then began to climb. They all watched him until the mist hid him from sight, then Bill Harris turned and looked at the water. 'I hope he hurries up,' he remarked.

Cassie was about to say, so do I, when she saw the grim expression on his face. 'What do you mean?'

'Look at the sea. The tide's coming in. And if you look at the seaweed on the cliffs you'll see that at high tide this bay is completely covered.'

'We can climb out, surely?'

'We can, perhaps, if there's a way up,' Bill agreed. 'But can she?' And he jerked his head towards Jeannie Cooper, who was leaning against the rocks, her eyes closed and her face very pale.

After that there didn't seem much to say until the pilot came back.

'I got to the top,' he told them. 'It's pretty tricky in one place, but we should be able to make it.'

'Any help up there?' Bill asked him, but hardly seemed surprised when he shook his head.

'No, none. Just open moorland, no roads or any sign of houses. Plenty of space for another chopper to land and pick us up, though, so I think we'd better try and get up there.' He looked across at Jeannie and then at Bill. 'You in much pain?'

'Can't feel a thing,' Bill replied in an obvious lie.

'Think you can help me with her?'

'Sure, but what about the baby?'

The pilot turned to Cassie, but she spoke before he

could even ask the question. 'Don't worry, I'll look after it, but I don't think I could climb up and carry it at the same time.'

'I don't want you to, I want you to just wait here until I come back for you. Okay?'

Cassie smiled at him. 'Okay.'

He grinned in response. 'Thanks, love. Right, let's try and rig something up so that I can carry her on my back.'

It was about twenty minutes before they set off, the pilot carrying Jeannie almost as a dead weight on his back with Bill Harris following behind to steady him. Even in that time the sea seemed to have come in a long way and had almost covered the helicopter. Cassie watched them slowly begin the climb and felt more alone than she'd ever felt in her life. Her thoughts flew to Simon, wondering if he was waiting for her and whether he yet knew that they'd crashed. Would he think that she'd been drowned? Would he perhaps be glad? The very thought chilled her more than her wet clothes, and she shivered violently.

The baby began to cry and she looked down at it, taking notice of it for the first time. She didn't know much about babies, but this one was, she supposed, quite a nice one; it wasn't all red and wrinkled like a monkey as most of them appeared to be. But it was so tiny; impossible to believe that anything that small could live. She'd forgotten to ask the mother how old it was, but it could only be a few days old at the most. It opened its mouth to cry again and she jiggled it up and down, not knowing what to do to keep it quiet. The poor little thing struggled in its blanket and its hands came out, bunched into minute fists as it beat at the air.

'Hush, hush! Don't cry, baby.' Cassie marvelled at its tiny hands, the fingers no bigger than her smallest fingernail but each one perfectly formed. She held it closer to her, tucking it inside her jacket, afraid its cry would carry to its mother and alarm her; it had been hard enough to persuade her to leave it behind as it was. The pilot had almost had to use violence in the end.

Tiny hands touched her breast, exploring, seeking, and she looked down and saw that the baby had its mouth open.

Cassie laughed softly. 'Oh, so you're hungry, are you? Well, you won't find anything there, chum—I'm not your mum. Here, try this.' Tentatively she put the joint of her bent little finger into the baby's mouth and he began to suck on it happily, his eyes closing in delight. Cassie stood looking down at the baby for a very long time, her eyes full of sadness.

Water lapping round her bare feet made her look up to see that the sea had reached the foot of the cliffs. There was no sign yet of the pilot coming back. It would have taken him a long time with Jeannie on his back, he would have had to take frequent rests, and then there was Bill; for all he said he was all right, he must have been in considerable pain, the pilot might even have had to leave him part way and then go back for him. They might even all be stuck up there somewhere.

Cassie waited until the water was up to her knees, then she buttoned the baby inside her jacket and held it firmly in place with one hand, then slowly began to climb the cliff at the spot where the others had gone up.

When the pilot came down he found her about fifteen feet up the cliff face, standing on a ledge and leaning against a protruding piece of rock, resting. He scrambled over to her and leant with her against the rock, getting his breath back.

'Sorry I took so long, had a bit of bother getting Mrs Cooper up the tricky bit.' He glanced down at the sea. 'Getting a bit wet down there, was it?'

'Just a bit,' Cassie agreed.

He grinned. 'We'll go on up in a minute. 'Fraid I'm a bit out of condition, I don't usually get this much exercise. How's the baby?'

'Asleep, I think.' Cassie glanced down at the child and settled it more comfortably in her arms. 'Are the others all right?'

'I don't think Bill Harris is very good—he passed out when we got to the top, that's another reason why I was so long, but at least looking after him is taking Mrs Cooper's mind off her baby. And another good thing is that the mist's lifting,' he added cheerfully.

He rested for a few minutes longer, than took off his jacket and shirt, putting the jacket back on and fashioning the shirt into a sort of sling for his back, into which they put the baby, rather like the North American Indians used to use.

'There, it should be all right in there for a bit.' He looked at Cassie quizzically. 'Ever done any rock-climbing?'

'No. But if you can get up there, I can.'

He smiled approvingly. 'Good girl! Just follow me and try and put your hands and feet where I do. If you get stuck or panicky just yell and I'll come back for you.'

They went up slowly, with several rests, for the pilot as much as Cassie; after climbing the cliff twice already he was wellnigh exhausted. Strangely enough the mist helped because they could only see the piece of cliff immediately around them, but it lifted as they neared the tricky bit, an overhang that had to be circumvented over loose, jagged rocks. Without shoes, Cassie found it extremely difficult. A piece of rock cut into her foot and she glanced down to look for a better foothold. She found herself looking down a sheer drop of fifty feet to the boiling sea and rocks below. Panic filled her and she gave a gasp of terror, clinging to the rock face, and too paralysed with fright to move.

Dimly above her she could hear the pilot calling her name, urging her on, but she couldn't move, could only weld herself to the cliff in an agony of fear.

Grimly he climbed back down to her. 'Come on, there's nothing to be afraid of. I'll hold you.' He tried to prize her fingers from where they were gripping a piece of rock, but Cassie moaned in fear and held on tighter than ever. His voice grew urgent. 'Come on, you've got to move. You're almost at the top. Come on,' he repeated. 'Your husband's waiting for you.'

Slowly Cassie's fingers unfroze. She moved a tentative hand upwards and began to climb again, the pilot encouraging and helping her. It seemed a thousand miles to the top, and even then she could hardly believe that they were safe until she crawled across the grass to where the others were waiting. Jeannie Cooper grabbed her baby and burst into tears. Cassie didn't blame her; she felt like having a good cry herself. She lay there for some time trying to still her pounding heart, then rolled over and saw that the mist had almost cleared and that, wonder of wonders, the grey cloud was breaking up and revealing patches of brilliant blue sky through which rays of golden sunlight were shafting down to the sea.

It was through one of these patches that they first saw the helicopter. They heard it first, then Jeannie Cooper gave an excited shout and pointed, and the pilot immediately sent up a flare. Then it seemed no time at all before the craft, from R.A.F. Rescue, had landed and picked them up, was taking them on to Kinray.

Cassie looked out of the window as they flew over the site, experiencing that Gulliver in Lilliput sensation again. They seemed to have progressed quite a lot since she had been here in February, two more of the jetties appeared to be completely finished. Simon's doing? she wondered. His drive and energy pushing the work on?

There were two ambulances waiting by the helicopter pad so that Jeannie Cooper and Bill Harris could be taken by stretcher and hurried away to the local cottage hospital. The pilot jumped out and she followed more slowly, her feet cut and sore. She grimaced wryly as she realised what she must look like, with her hair loose and windswept, her clothes torn and sea-stained. One of the R.A.F. men went to lift her down, but then he was shouldered aside and Simon was there.

He was staring up at her, his face white and drawn, more haggard than she had ever seen it. He said urgently, 'Cassie,' then reached up and lifted her down. For a long moment he gazed into her face, then he made a small sound in his throat and pulled her roughly into his arms to hold her very, very tightly. Neither of them moved or spoke for some time, both too choked by emotion to do more than just cling to each other.

But then Simon put his hands up to her face and asked unsteadily, 'Are you—are you all right?'

She nodded and tried to smile. 'Yes. Except that I—I lost my shoes.'

He glanced down at her feet, then stooped to pick her up in his arms. There was a car waiting nearby and he carried her across, ignoring a doctor who wanted her to go to hospital for a check-up and some reporters who tried to ask questions and take pictures. After putting her in the passenger seat, Simon got in beside her and drove firmly through the crowd of people, accelerating out of the oil terminal and along the road to his house. Cassie leant back in the seat, content just to look at him, knowing that this wasn't the time for words. Not yet. That time was still to come, but now it wasn't so important any more.

At the house he lifted her out of the car and carried her upstairs to the bedroom. No one came to see who it was; they had the place to themselves. He set her down and helped her to take off her ruined jacket and skirt, then knelt and gently took off her torn tights. Cassie couldn't help a tremor running through her as she felt his hands on her legs, and his eyes came swiftly up to meet hers. But then he helped her into a chair, went into the bathroom, and coming back with a bowl of warm water began very tenderly to bathe her feet, then dry them on a soft towel.

Cassie sat in the chair, her eyes closed, feeling drained of strength and emotion. That there was still a great gulf between them she knew, but for the moment she thrust all thoughts of it aside, feeling only his hands tending her, taking care of her, knowing that he was close.

Simon moved away and she slowly opened her eyes. He was standing watching her, the drawn look still in his face but not so pale now.

Cassie tensed nervously and sat up, her eyes large and troubled. 'Simon, I . . .'

But her words were broken off as he bent suddenly and caught her by the arms, pulling her to her feet. He kissed her then, so fiercely that he hurt her, bending her head back so that she had to cling to him to stop herself falling. And then his hands were at her clothes, pulling them off, clumsy in his haste. She tried to speak, but he silenced her with his mouth, picking her up and carrying her over to the bed.

He stood looking down at her, his breathing unsteady. 'Oh God, I'd almost forgotten how beautiful you are.' His hand came down to touch her breast and she shuddered and gasped.

Simon began to pull off his clothes, throwing them down anyhow, and then he was beside her on the bed, pulling her to him.

Suddenly there was so much Cassie wanted to say, wanted to tell him before he made love to her, so that everything was straight between them. She got as far as, 'Simon, please let me . . .' but he mistook what she was going to say and stopped her roughly.

'No,' he said savagely, 'I'm not going to let you go. Now or ever. You're *mine*, Cassie. You belong to me. And I should have done this weeks ago!'

He took her then, with a savage hunger, his need for her so urgent that there was no time for gentleness. Cassie moved under him, taking his body as fiercely as he gave it, wanting him so badly, her insides on fire with passion and desire. She dug her nails into his back, crying out his name, her body arching under him as she felt his body shudder with pleasure, and ecstasy engulfed her. They lay, then, clinging to each other, panting and breathless, their bodies burning hot, but it had been so long since they had been together that soon Simon's hands and mouth were on her, touching, kissing, and Cassie was moaning, 'Love me again. Oh, Simon, please, please love me again!'

He was more gentle this time, lifting her to the heights of desire and holding her there until she cried out for him and pulled him fiercely down on top of her, giving herself to him in complete surrender.

Afterwards they lay together, their bodies for the moment exhausted but still very close together. Cassie's cheeks were wet with tears of joy and gratitude and Simon tenderly kissed them away. He looked into her face searchingly, his fingers gently exploring every feature all over again. When they reached her mouth he grew still, then said fiercely, 'I meant it, Cassie, I'm not going to let you go! It doesn't matter what happened between you and Tom. Not any more. God, when I thought that you'd been killed . . .' He broke off, his face twisted in remembered pain.

Quickly Cassie put her hands on either side of his face. 'Simon, listen to me. There was nothing between Tom and me. I was never unfaithful to you.'

His eyes flew to meet hers, incredulous, vulnerable. 'You're not just saying that to . . .'

'No! Oh, okay, we kissed a couple of times, but when he asked me to go to bed with him I said no. I—I couldn't, you see.'

Simon tensed and his hand tightened. 'I saw you together, Cassie.' He didn't say it accusingly, almost sadly.

'All you saw,' Cassie said urgently, 'was Tom dropping me off at the flat. I hadn't been with him that weekend—I'd gone away alone to try and think things out. You can check with the hotel where I was staying, if you don't believe me. I phoned him and asked him to pick me up at the station when I got back to London because I—well, because I'd made up my mind that I wasn't going to see him any more.'

'You mean . . .'

Steadily Cassie said, 'I told him that night. He wouldn't accept it at first, but in the end he had to.'

'Oh, Cassie!' A look of relief and thankfulness came into Simon's eyes. 'If you only knew how hard it's been to try and live with the thought of you together, of you in another man's arms.'

'Don't! Oh, please don't. I'm sorry, Simon. I've been such a fool. But I was so lonely. I missed you so much!'

He pulled her to him almost violently and held her tightly in his arms. 'We've both been damn fools, me more than you. I thought that if we loved each other enough we could weather any separation, any problems. But it was wrong of me to expect so much.'

'No, you weren't wrong. It was my fault. I was so lonely without you that I got angry and wanted to hurt you. But really it was just saying that I needed you. You see, I missed you so much, Simon, so very much.'

'Darling!' He kissed her gently, but then frowned and said, 'But if you'd decided to end it with Tom, why did you say you wanted a divorce? Because I jumped to the wrong conclusion?'

'Partly that,' Cassie paused and added with difficulty, 'and partly because you were with a woman when I phoned you.'

'With a woman?' Simon's eyebrows flew up in incredulous surprise.

'Yes. I heard her start to speak and then stop.'

Simon began to laugh. 'You adorable idiot—that was

the television news. I switched it off with the remote control.'

'You mean I've been tormented by jealousy because of a news announcer? Oh, Simon!' Cassie clung to him as he laughed again.

'I'm glad you were jealous,' he murmured. 'I want you always to be jealous.' He bent to touch her lips with his, exploring her mouth with tantalising little kisses, then moving on to trace the curve of her cheek, her throat, her eyes, coming back to her mouth with ravenous hunger. 'Oh, God, Cassie, I love you. No matter what it takes, we're never going to be parted again.'

He went to kiss her again, but Cassie stopped him, looking up at him searchingly. 'Would you really have given me a divorce?'

He smiled and carried her hand to his lips, kissing her fingertips. 'No, but I was getting pretty desperate by then. That's why I insisted that you come up here. I realised what a stubborn fool I'd been and that the only chance we had of getting back together was here, in this bed.'

Cassie laughed a little. 'So this is where I would have ended up anyway?'

'Most definitely.' Simon looked down at her, his face suddenly serious again. His voice raw with emotion, he said, 'You see, you're the most precious thing in my life, and there was no way I could let you go.'

Cassie stared up at him, overwhelmed and feeling strangely humbled, but then, as he began to kiss and caress every curve of her body, awaken each sexual nerve end one by one, she was again lost in passion, her body responding to his touch as he made love to her again and again, until they both fell into a long, contented sleep.

It was daylight before she awoke and for a few seconds she thought she was in the flat, alone in bed as she had been for so long, and the familiar desolation filled her heart, but then she moved and felt Simon's naked body beside her. Recollection and joy flooded through her in a wave so great she thought she would burst with happiness. It was all right. They were together again and everything was going to be fine from now on. Carefully she turned so that she could see him, savouring this moment of pure happiness to try and hold it for ever in her mind. She wanted to reach out and touch him, to trace the outline of his hard jaw and straight nose, to smooth away the beginnings of a grim line at the corner of his mouth that had never been there before. But she was afraid to wake him, wanting to hold on to this moment for ever.

She lay still until quite a while later when he moved and turned on to his back, then she glanced at the clock on the bedside table, sat up and reached for the phone. She asked the operator to get her the local cottage hospital and then asked the matron on duty how Bill Harris and Jeannie Cooper were.

'Och,' the woman replied in a broad Scots accent, 'they're both fine. We're keeping Mr Harris in for a day or two, but Mrs Cooper will be away home today.'

'And her child?'

'The bairn's fine. Not a thing wrong with him.'

'I'm so glad. Will you please tell them that Mrs Ventris called.'

She put the receiver down slowly, remembering those few hours of danger that had brought a group of strangers so close together, only to part again when they were safe. Turning, she saw that Simon was awake and watching her.

'Are they all right?'

'Yes, fine.'

He held out his hand to her, but she surprised him by saying determinedly, 'Simon, are you very busy at the oil terminal? Can you take a few days off?'

He smiled rather wryly. 'Of course. I'll be giving it up anyway to come back to London with you.'

Cassie gazed at him as the import of his words struck home and she became fully aware of the sacrifice he was willing to make to keep her. Then she smiled and slipped down into bed to snuggle up to him. 'That won't be necessary.'

His eyebrows rose. 'It won't?'

'No, because of the heavy schedule you've got over the next few days.' She moved against him voluptuously, arousing him at once.

'What heavy schedule?' Simon asked thickly as he reached for her.

'Making quite sure you give me a baby.'

His fingers bit into her flesh so hard that she gasped.

'*What* did you say?' His grey eyes stared into hers. 'Do you mean it? Oh, God, Cassie are you sure?'

'Yes,' Cassie answered softly, putting up a hand to stroke his face. 'I did quite a lot of thinking when I was stuck on that beach, and I'm very sure.'

'But what about your career?'

'It will just have to wait until your job here is finished and the baby's old enough to go to nursery school. If Marriott & Brown's won't take me back, I'll open a shop of my own. In the meantime we'll just be together, here in Scotland. Because all I want is to be with you.'

'Oh, Cassie! My darling girl!' He held her very close for a long time, until Cassie moved restlessly and he loosened his hold.

She looked at him impatiently. 'Well, what are you waiting for? You do want the job I'm offering, don't you?'

Simon laughed, a deep, masculine laugh of pure happiness. 'I most certainly do. And I'll do my very best to give satisfaction, ma'am.' And he did.

The bestselling epic saga of the Irish. An intriguing and passionate story that spans 400 years.

FIRST...

The Defiant

Lady Elizabeth Hatton, highborn
Englishwoman, was not above using
her position to get what she wanted
...and more than anything in the
world she wanted Rory
O'Donnell, the fiery Irish rebel.
But it was an alliance that promised
only ruin....

THEN...

The Survivors

Against a turbulent background of
political intrigue and royal
corruption, the determined,
passionate Shanna O'Hara searched
for peace in her beloved
but troubled Ireland. Meanwhile
in England, hot-tempered
Brenna Coke fought against
a loveless marriage....

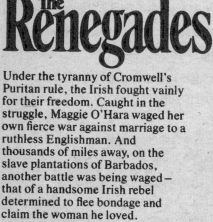

Romance Treasury

Your chance to collect beautiful early editions!

Each Romance Treasury volume is a delightful anthology of three favorite Harlequin Romances all by bestselling authors of romantic fiction. Handsomely bound in gold-embossed leatherette hard covers, with colorfully illustrated jackets, these attractive volumes are an asset to any home library!

Choose from the list of great volumes on the following page.

Choose from this list of
Romance Treasury editions

**Complete and mail coupon
on following page today!**

Collect a love-story library with
Romance Treasury

Complete and mail this coupon today!

Harlequin Reader Service

In the U.S.A.
1440 South Priest Drive
Tempe, AZ 85281

In Canada
649 Ontario Street,
Stratford, Ontario N5A 6W2

Please send me the following Romance Treasuries. I am enclosing
my check or money order for $6.97 for each Treasury ordered plus
75¢ to cover postage and handling.

□ *Volume 5*   □ *Volume 61*

□ *Volume 10*   □ *Volume 64*

□ *Volume 41*   □ *Volume 67*

□ *Volume 48*   □ *Volume 70*

□ *Volume 52*   □ *Volume 74*

Number of Treasuries checked @ $6.97 each = $_____

N.Y. and Ariz. residents add appropriate sales
tax. $_____

Postage and handling $_____ 75¢

I enclose   TOTAL $_____

(Please send check or money order. We cannot be responsible for cash sent through
the mail.)
Prices subject to change without notice.

NAME_____

ADDRESS_____
                                            (APT. NO.)

CITY_____

STATE/PROVINCE_____

ZIP/POSTAL CODE_____
Order while quantities last. This offer expires April 30, 1983   2105600000C